Concierge
SERVICE
★ ★ ★ ★ ★
P.D. SINGER

ROCKY RIDGE BOOKS

Concierge Service

Cover art by Kellie Dennis of Book Cover by Design

Edited by Eden Winters

ISBN-13 978-1-62622-051-5

Published by:

Rocky Ridge Books
PO Box 6922
Broomfield, CO 80021
www.RockyRidgeBooks.com

What readers say about P.D. Singer's work:

A New Man is one of the best love stories I've ever read. The transformation of Chad's personality is brilliantly written. I'm not sure anyone less talented than Ms. Singer could have pulled this one off.

Becky Condit, USA Today, *A New Man*

The chemistry between Lee and Bobby is off the charts. And that is without any physical shenanigans. Just watching them work together, get reacquainted, and chase a historical legend was breathtaking.

Rainbow Book Reviews, *Diving Deep*

This is a terrific read and I hope you treat yourself by picking it up. It's an intelligent, interesting, emotionally satisfying story with lovable characters.

Gay Book Reviews, *Spokes*

This story is extraordinary, with characters that are immensely complex and pacing that is so fast I felt as if I were riding a wave that kept on building. I admired the author's ingenuity, audacity and skill in writing a story based on the money markets that evolved into an exciting adventure and love story.

Reviews by Jessewave, *The Rare Event*

Overall, this book was simply delightful. The mix of quiet moments and tense action scenes made this a real page turner…

Reviews by Jessewave, *Blood on the Mountain*

Many thanks are due to Eden Winters, TD O'Malley,
Angela Benedetti, Kayla Jameth, and Kate Pavelle,
who cheered or kicked my butt as needed.
Thanks to Scott Pavelle, who provided a critical plot point.

Also thanks to Devyn Morgan, for letting me borrow Rory.
I returned him in good shape.

Concierge

SERVICE

★ ★ ★ ★ ★

P.D. SINGER

Chapter One

The tapping of dress oxfords and high heels along the brown and white marble chessboard of a floor signaled mid-afternoon check-in at the Vivaldi Central Park. Some of those shoes belonged to the guests, others to the various personal assistants who kept their wealthy employers from soiling their fingers with something as mundane as a hotel registry.

Did the guests appreciate the cut-glass bowls arcing light beneath the heavy cream froth of ranunculus and fuchsia-edged gentians? Or would the next privileged couple to come through complain of the flowers' lack of scent? Even though the blooms had been carefully chosen to not offend the allergy sufferers in the clientele. The low strains of baroque violin blurred the conversations in seven languages at the front desk, the concierge desk, and the bell captain's kiosk.

The heat that persisted into late September stayed outside—it wasn't welcome in the cool, hushed hotel lobby, any more than were guests not inclined to spend four figures per night for a place to be seen, be talked about, perchance to sleep. A high-rise at Park Avenue and 58 th Street in midtown Manhattan should not be mistaken for a Holiday Inn.

The "I have people for that" crowd seldom handed over their own credit cards to stay at this landmark five-star hotel, but they were quite good at making requests. The reasonable to outlandish ratio was running skewed towards reasonable today. Joshua Hannes withdrew two tickets for *Hamilton* for the guests in 411 and pocketed the hundred-dollar tip with a smile for the acknowledgement of his services.

He'd earned the tip twice over—the musical had been sold out for months. The guests casually asked only this morning, and it had taken Joshua three phone calls and one favor to produce seats for the following night. Quite the bargain at three hundred bucks a head. Joshua resisted the urge to polish his already highly-buffed nails on his lapel and stroke his dark waves into satisfied perfection.

"It can't last, Lauren," murmured Joshua. "Nothing but dry cleaning, theater tickets, dinner reservations and one dog walker. Nobody's asked for a table for breakfast at Tiffany's yet."

His partner at the concierge desk shot off a text to someone who'd appear at the side door, stay long enough to perform some essential service—or "essential" service, one that normal people did for themselves and those who used designer toilet paper hired out, and ran fingers through her straight blonde bob. "Tiffany's really missed the boat by not opening a tea room sooner. We could have kept them packed all these years."

"Who needs a concierge when you have Holly Golightly?" If Joshua had a fiver for every tourist who'd asked for that previously impossible reservation, he'd be wearing Brioni instead of Boss. "Oh, by the way, the manager from Spoons called, said we should come by for breakfast."

"You go." Lauren twirled her pen. "I hate getting up early on a morning off."

Joshua grinned. "That's because you'd rather refresh restauranteurs' memories over dinner."

Lauren reached over to straighten the knot on Joshua's tie, a vintage Countess Mara in icy blue slubbed silk with an embroidered monogram, not Joshua's. She had to reach up quite a way—she was petite and he stood six feet tall. "And a good cabernet."

"Of course." Recommending restaurants where he hadn't sampled the food was a rookie move—and if the owner wanted to sweeten a concierge's memory with a bottle of something luscious, Joshua didn't mind at all. Even if he only shared it with Lauren or one of their other colleagues.

The phone rang—he was a trifle faster and got the call, on an outside line. "Vivaldi Central Park, concierge desk, this is Joshua."

The voice coming through the phone could have been fine burgundy or twenty-year old scotch. "This is Craig Ridley. I need to let you know I'll be late checking in. Not sure if the reservation is under Ridley or SecurNow. And I was wondering what sort of kosher meals are available anywhere near the hotel."

Definitely a tourist. If he could imagine a kosher dish, someone in Manhattan served it. "Are you thinking fine dining, homey, or more of a deli experience, Mr. Ridley?"

"Whoa, there's kosher fine dining?" Incredulity blew through the earpiece and turned into lust on the way to

Joshua's groin. That voice…. "I figured mom and pop places at most, and not in the vicinity."

Joshua managed not to laugh, and he'd say anything to keep talking to this guest who had a voice for radio. Possibly a face for radio too, but he could keep dreaming until he actually got a look. "This is New York City, Mr. Ridley. If you want it, I can get it for you."

Too late he realized how that sounded. Please let the guest not want anything to put up his nose or anyone to wrap around his dick. "If it's legit."

"Of course." Ridley laughed. "Does that mean you bring it in, or make reservations, or…?"

"Whichever you prefer," Joshua answered smoothly, carefully not meeting Lauren's eyes. Educating the new-to-the-city guests on just what a good concierge could accomplish was a daily task, and if he caught her mouthing some of their favorite lines, he'd burst. "Would you like meals brought in?"

"I was expecting to live on pastrami on rye, so, yes." His joy wafted through the airwaves. "I didn't realize that was possible."

Another voice, feminine, also wafted through, more faintly. "If you wanted a bottle of fifty-year old Glenfiddich, three M&Ms in a row on the side table, and a towel animal, he'd get them. Or a hooker."

"How… interesting," went off to the side. "Um, I'd be happy with, ah, I don't want to go down the menu item by item. What's good there?"

Which "there"? Joshua had three places in mind, although he'd only seen one of the chefs recently. Bearing a covered dish of foodgasm-inducing noms—Joshua could make this recommendation whole-heartedly. "Mikeleh's does an amazing beef short rib."

"Sounds good, short ribs it is, pick a salad and a side, and, ah… a bottle of Rhone." Tired notes crept into the velvet baritone caressing Joshua's ear. "For eight o'clock, please."

"One dinner of short ribs, and will there be anything else?" Joshua meant, "for your companion," but apparently Ridley intended to dine alone.

"No. Oh wait, yes." A chuckle that went all the way down to Joshua's toes could signal either a boner-killer or a dream-catcher. "I'd like a towel animal on the bed. Folder's choice."

"Of course." Joshua wouldn't say no to anything a guest wanted, even if he hadn't the faintest idea—yet—how to procure it. Especially not to a guest so delighted with a small service, and who sounded like sex walking. Money wasn't everything—a little dream fuel didn't hurt at all. It would come crashing down soon enough, like right after the call ended.

Or sooner. Joshua took down the credit card information, and the end of his fantasy.

"And whatever hearty spinach salad they have. Right, Felicity?"

"Perfect," she agreed in the background.

No, that wasn't perfect at all.

Chapter Two

At seven p.m. Ridley still hadn't checked in, but dinner was to be at eight. With one eye on the clock, the other on the front desk, and requests coming in, Joshua juggled his pen, his phone, and his nerves. "Almond pastries, the square kind from Giroud's, and decaf, seven-thirty sharp," he assured the lady in 304, knowing that this trip, like every other, she wouldn't accept the round almond pastries from the hotel kitchen. Perhaps the sight of the white box picked with gold foil lettering held some precious memory of her past.

Joshua wouldn't question, he'd leave a memo for a bellman to run the four long blocks to the fancy bakery in time for 304's breakfast. If she wanted square pastries, that's what she'd get.

Everyone was happy, except for Joshua, who dared not wait any longer to feed a possible no-show. Ridley hadn't specified "eight o'clock or when I get here" so Joshua wouldn't delay. He phoned the order in, dispatched one of the bellmen to fetch it, and caught the eye of the front desk clerk.

"Which room are you putting Craig Ridley in?" he asked Tyler.

"Don't know yet." Tyler let a forelock of curls swing over his eyes. He turned to the counter, suddenly interested in the alignment of pens against keyboard.

"Don't give me that." Joshua aimed a gimlet glare at the front desk agent. "Where are you putting him?"

"I really don't know." The glare was mostly lost on the redhead, although the laser force should have the tips of his ringlets smoking. "We're oversold."

"Damn it, are you going to have to send him over to the Marcel?" Visions of cold beef and shaken red wine danced before Joshua's eyes. "The guy's tired, hungry, and expecting our best, which he is paying lavishly for."

"I know." Tyler rearranged the pens horizontally. "But the only room left is the Central Park Suite, and he reserved a standard king."

"Then put him in the Central Park Suite." Was this blindingly obvious only to Joshua? "Would you rather upgrade him or send him away unhappy? Never to return?"

"Upgrade him, but…" Tyler peeked out from behind his curls. "We're talking a two-bedroom penthouse suite versus a run of the house king. That's a pretty big upgrade."

Time was ticking, and Tyler argued? "You can make or lose a client for life with this."

"I know, but…"

Joshua leaned close to Tyler's ear. "How about you make up your mind and I won't tell the general manager who's been soothing his pain with the Grey Goose miniatures the minibar guy's always coming up short on?"

"Damn it, Josh!" Tyler blurted. "You're asking me to authorize a two thousand dollar a night upgrade."

"I know. But I also know nobody else has that suite booked until the end of the month, and if it goes unsold this week, you can't ever go back and sell it to someone else." Joshua leaned forward, one eye on the red and gray livery of a bellman visible through the smoked glass picture windows, headed to the front door. He balanced a red thermal pack like a pizza in one hand and dangled a white plastic bag from the other. Joshua *had* to have a table to lay out the Ridleys' dinner. "How about you upgrade him, I say nothing to Grant, *and* you can take your problem boyfriend to breakfast at Spoons?"

"Whoa, you mean that?" Tyler blinked. "We've never been able to get in that joint!"

Probably not. Tyler and Problem Boyfriend either didn't stop fighting early enough or get up early enough to eat trendy waffles. "Sure. I have an invite, you're going to go in my place, *if* you put Ridley in the suite, right now, because I need to go organize their dinner." Joshua leaned in again, gripping Tyler's elbow. "Got me?"

"Gotcha!" Tyler started tapping on his keyboard.

Good, because if Joshua wasn't mistaken, the power couple in business suits emerging from the limo right in front of the hotel were the tired, hungry people whose dinner he had to intercept. He snagged a master key card from Tyler's drawer and bolted. Wouldn't do to be caught with service half done!

"Thanks!" Joshua pounced on Henry, lounging at the concierge desk, trying to shoot the breeze with an unimpressed Lauren, who probably didn't really have anyone on the other end of that phone call. Joshua had his own reasons for not talking to the slimeball. Lauren had told him to fuck off just as vividly.

"Heya, Josh." Henry smirked. "Got a call for a handsome young man such as yourself."

"Not happening," Joshua snapped, too low to be heard by anyone not standing at the desk. "Fuck off," he meant but it didn't do to antagonize a bellman. They had too many ways of getting even. If Henry suggested adding Joshua to his stable of "extra pillows" one more time, it might be time to test the industrial trash compactor in the back alley.

Not that he wanted to repay the insult with a tip, but Henry had fetched, and there was a method to the way the staff worked. Joshua stuffed a ten-dollar bill into Henry's hand, snatched the thermal pack and bag, and blew through the lobby to the elevator, which, please, Lord, don't make it stop on every single floor this time.

Maybe Tyler would feel beholden enough for the gratis meal to take a few extra minutes to describe all the amenities that came with the unexpected upgrade. Or maybe he'd be pissy enough to skip mentioning some of the nicer perks that plumped the suite's price into the stratosphere.

Like the chauffeured Rolls Royce. Joshua needed to find out, before he promised anything contradictory, because Tyler might decide keeping the Rolls off the table would soothe the GM into smiling about selling the suite for the price of a king. Joshua would have to soothe the GM himself, maybe with a couple of those Davidoff Perfectos he'd picked up for less than $80 a cigar. There was a reason he'd bought more than he'd acquired for the hotel humidor. Never knew when you'd need a favor.

If he didn't have the towel animal folded before the Ridleys came upstairs… His pride required something more complicated than a snake. Joshua balanced his phone on the thermal pack, poking up a YouTube video demonstrating something simple. He spent the fifty-three-floor ride studying how to assemble an elephant from a bath towel and a hand towel—how hard could this be?

Better be as easy as the demo made it look—Joshua was running out of time. He laid the table in the dining area, leaving the food packaged lest the short ribs go cold, and dove into the bathroom. A guy could get lost in here between the mirrors endlessly reflecting the warm, golden-veined Italian marble that seemed to cover everything but the ceiling. He seized the towels and set to work rolling an elephant in the master bedroom.

Well, okay, Dumbo needed a squint to come alive, but it was an elephant, it was mostly symmetrical. This suite had two bedrooms. Not that he expected a couple who'd booked a king to use them both, but a job well done beat the hell out of a job half done. The second elephant went faster. Joshua let himself out of the suite, the only unit on the entire floor, just in time to meet the couple at the elevator. Henry followed with a cart of luggage.

Joshua nodded politely. "Dinner with elephants, sir. Madame."

Madame barely glanced his way, and only because the furniture talked.

"Thank you." Craig Ridley—who else could it be with that smooth, deep voice? Oh man, a face and body to match, early to mid-thirties, with a dress sense to kill for—nodded in return, reaching to shake Joshua's hand. The crinkle of bills rustled against his palm, to be ignored even after the elevator closed its burnished bronze doors around him.

Joshua hated to even look at his tip, because nothing Craig Ridley or his unfairly female companion could give him would ever make up for the monstrous iniquity of Craig not being gay.

Chapter Three

Unpacking the suitcases might be a little *too* much pampering for Craig Ridley's taste. Passing over a discretely folded bill, he shooed the bellman out before the first lock could be unlatched. Craig didn't want strangers handling his underwear, or what was wrapped in them.

Wow, this suite! He'd been pretty sure he understood luxury, but a living room, dining room, an en-suite bathroom that looked more like a spa, a second bath, and two bedrooms was more than he imagined needing in a hotel room. More than he'd considered even existing, really, since the living room looked more like an art gallery with a baby grand piano. Was that a real Kandinsky on the wall? Might be—it was no print, not with the swirls and globs of paint raised above the canvas. The signature might be a fake, but that was a real Steinway silhouetted against the spectacular light show of mid-town Manhattan. The city looked very different from the fifty-third floor.

Craig prowled from room to room, stunned. "This suite defines conspicuous consumption. Good God. For one person?"

"Or two or four." Felicity had given the suite a once-over from the dining area and turned her attention to setting out the food. When he emerged from the master bedroom the third time, she waved her fork at him. "Really, Craig, if you can have nice things, why not have them?"

"I suppose. I'm just not used to thinking in terms of *this* nice, for me." He fell into more than sat in the dining chair and picked up his fork. "That smells so good." One bite later— "Oh, that *is* good. I didn't realize how hungry I'd gotten."

"So hungry you didn't check the packaging on the food."

Craig froze, his fork halfway to his mouth.

"Don't worry, I did." Felicity always looked after him. "Mikeleh's, fine kosher dining, all over the wrappers."

Oh good—he could eat.

Felicity took another bite of salad as if he had no reason to panic. "I'm glad you didn't insist on deli. I tire of brown mustard after a meal or two."

Whatever this grain and mushroom side dish was, Craig wanted more. He wanted more of any dish this restaurant served, and he'd be here all week. He could use the menu for food porn, easy. He could start at the top and work his way down. "Me too, but better safe than sorry."

"I suppose, though it does get a little old for the rest of us." She took a sip of the red wine.

"If this is the worst eccentricity you have to put up with from me, I think you'll survive, lady." He jabbed into his plate with the clatter of silver against china. "Since surviving is at the top of my personal to-do list."

Patting the air, *down, boy, down,* with her free hand, Felicity tried to soothe him. "Yes, of course, it is. If you do want deli, you can trust this concierge to get it from a proper kosher deli, not the nearest Jewish-style deli. A five-star hotel understands pickiness."

Well, hell, Craig wasn't soothed. "Wouldn't it be nice if this were a matter of pickiness? I can only wish that's all it was." He bit into a forkful of beef as if it had personally offended him, and had to issue a mental apology to the chef for swallowing without tasting.

"Yes, I know, Craig. I do remember the last time," she snapped. "Vividly."

"Not as vividly as I do." He stabbed at the meat instead of her. "If you'd like to make your first fifty million, maybe you should just indulge my 'pickiness' instead of bitching."

"The first fifty million I made myself, friend. I was born with my first fifty million." She patted her lips with her napkin, which hid her next jab not at all. "So I knew which fork to use before I was thirty."

"Apparently Miss Manners didn't teach you one damned thing about compassion." He dropped his fork on a plate of food gone suddenly bland. "Didn't you say you were going to spend the night with your sister? You could entertain yourselves by snapping your fingers at the help. Again."

"That once was an error of judgment." She threw her napkin down next to her plate. "But yes, I am going over to my sister's, where I expect to enjoy civilized companionship suitable for a Van de Bogart."

"We'll both enjoy the evening more if you do." Craig rose, anxious to be rid of this brittle, overgroomed harpy in a skirt. "I'll see you at the bank in the morning, with your happy money face on."

Felicity had never seemed so poorly named. She snarled on her way across the living room toward the door. "I do not have to put up with this, Craig. I'm leaving."

If he opened the door for her, he could shove her out and close it behind her. "Perhaps you should remember, that as far as SecurNow and I are concerned, Felicity, you are the help.

Chapter Four

The rest of his meal tasted the finer for lack of criticism.

Fed, but caught in the weird limbo of exhausted and wired, Craig paced around his lush temporary domain. Another exploration of the secondary bedroom brought out a detail he'd missed before.

He picked up the towel elephant, trying to figure out how it was put together without unrolling it. Nice. Craig had only asked for one, out of the sheer whimsy of being able to make such a nonsensical request and having it fulfilled. The guy who'd rolled and tucked this little critter into existence had not only left one on the master bed, but had gone the extra mile to leave one in here, too. Thorough.

Craig admired that in a man.

The man himself was easy on the eye, tall and lean, with a shock of brunet hair that would look wonderful tousled, even better than neatly combed.

Which was a thought for the spank bank, and not going to do him a lick of good now.

The spank bank hardly ever had deposits.

Did jet lag do bad things to the brain? Here he was, indulging in a fantasy of a stranger about whom he knew nothing more than the man was thorough. Maybe he couldn't make conversation past the latest celebrity gossip. Or he could have a partner. Maybe the long drought since the last truly interesting man had crossed Craig's path was making his imagination work overtime.

Whatever, it wasn't like he'd have the opportunity to find out, which at least attached to the privilege of skipping the argument over attraction. He'd been called "unbefuckinglievably picky" a few too many times by men he'd found unbefuckinglievably ready to drop trou without knowing one damn thing about him, let alone liking or respecting anything beyond his face and his bank account. Skip that whole mess and the concierge could remain a pleasant thought.

He flicked through four movies, hating each one within a scene or two. He could go out, but that involved shoes. He could play the Steinway, but three rousing renditions of Chopsticks exhausted his repertory.

Anyone he wanted to talk to was two time zones away, probably putting the kids to bed or catching up on the cuddles they'd missed while they were scrambling to get this IPO put together.

Craig hadn't missed any cuddles, or he'd missed all the cuddles from a someone who wasn't part of his life. He needed to meet somebody, like that was possible.

This particular bit of craziness would be over in a week, but the nuttiness that came from running the company and doing the social things that went with running the company weren't going away. Try finding someone who understood that. A fuck buddy didn't get to question it, but Craig doubted he could even get it up for any man he had so little regard for. He could scratch his own damn itches, but if he started talking to himself...

Maybe that was the answer—unwind with one of the toys he'd dragged along from Denver this morning. He unpacked his suitcase, eyeing the bottle of lube. Did hotel guests ever ask the concierge to fetch another, or more toys? Not a request Craig could see himself making.

No, he didn't want to give himself a solitary hand job—he wanted to talk to someone. See a friendly face. Someone who wouldn't accidentally turn the conversation back to equity and shares and total float and lockout time, and how much more would they be worth when... Someone not associated with work. Or his usual life.

He eyed the sleek black house phone on the bedside table.

Naw. Too ridiculous. Too late.

Twenty-four/seven concierge service, whispered the memory of the redheaded twink at Reception. And the concierge on the phone: *If you want it, I can get it for you.*

Oh, hell. The worst they could say was no.

"That was weird." Lauren returned the phone to its cradle, one eyebrow quirked up high.

"If you're calling it weird, they must have wanted a 55-gallon drum of lube and a mini-trampoline. Or a table at the Trough." Joshua dragged his thoughts back from the horse-drawn carriage ride around Central Park for the couple in 1710 for tomorrow, rose petals to be strewn on the floor and bed for room 608, and a pair of Christian Louboutin sandals in gold metallic for the trophy wife in

3902, who swore him to secrecy on her shoe size. None of those were high effort requests, and not nearly enough to keep his mind off the vision in the penthouse suite who was eating dinner with and then going to bed with someone who was not Joshua.

"Seriously, that was weird. Never had a request like that before." Lauren pulled out her tablet and made a note. "Where do you get a 55-gallon drum of lube, anyway?"

"Amazon. Three-day shipping, so plan ahead, figure it will run you about two grand, sell it for three grand. Plan on bribing two bellmen to help you get it upstairs and into the bathtub, extra if it's Henry, to keep him from trying it out. Shithead." Joshua had not forgotten that memorable "romantic evening" he'd arranged for a hotel guest. Nor had Housekeeping forgotten who masterminded that incredible mess—Amaya and Paolina still muttered darkly under their breaths about *el pato* who made so much extra work. He'd stuck to recommending the rose petals on the bed after that. "If it's a rush job, try one of the bigger sex shops in the West Village and figure on double the cost."

"Great, haven't been asked for that, but you never know." She completed her note and closed the app.

Joshua glanced around for any listeners, but the lobby was empty save for a couple waiting for an elevator, Tyler at reception who was absorbed in texting, and Henry, who hadn't perked up at the sound of his name. Joshua spoke quietly all the same—part of Lauren's phone call had included, "The bellman has extra pillows in your choice of ethnicities," in tones cold enough to grow icicles on bystanders' dicks.

She shifted from foot to foot and finally opted to slip

out of her stylish shoes. "It was your kosher towel guy in the penthouse. He wanted—"

Oh great, the hottie with the sexy rumble was a perv. Goodbye, tonight's fantasy.

She chuckled. "It was kind of sweet and naïve, if it was for real. He swore he wasn't asking for a hooker, he wanted someone to talk to, play Scrabble or something, all innocent. Someone to talk to. Said to 'think Rent-a-friend.' Because he was alone."

"What happened to the elegant woman in the suit who came in with him?" Weird was right—was there some sort of kinky game waiting to unfold five hundred feet above his head?

Lauren yawned—they had twenty minutes left to go on their shift. "Saw her leave a while ago. My gawd, that woman can put her nose in the air. Thought she was going to walk right over the Hunters. The doorman put her in a cab. I think you were off raiding for rose petals."

"Hey, recycling at its finest. All those flowers would just go to waste after the banquet if I didn't give them a second life." Joshua'd filled a garbage sack of full of used centerpieces, which he'd stuffed into their storeroom to strip in his leisure moments. Their perfume wafted under the door behind the concierge desk, the scent of happiness for romantics. He had at least one Romeo in the hotel, and likely another one or two this weekend—those roses wouldn't have a chance to wilt before their final performance.

Also, good riddance to Felicity McSnooterson.

Fantasy reactivated.

And "rent-a-friend"?

Joshua's heartbeat kicked up and other body parts wanted in on the action.

Alone. In a room. With the hottest man ever to check into Joshua's hotel.

All in the name of good service, too!

Not that anything would happen.

Joshua ducked back into their storeroom, where shelves crammed with the trinkets and luxuries often requested lined the walls. Hmm, should be on the bottom shelf, far right…

No. Oh right, the family traveling with the tween daughter took the Scrabble board with them. He should have replaced it a week ago, but the twelve-pack of playing cards should still be there. Yes! A deck of cards, and… Something non-alcoholic, nothing to imply this was a date, or assignation. Yes, a six-pack of trendy, effervescent juice drinks lurked in the fridge next to seven kinds of chocolates from three different countries. Some folks just couldn't be happy with the hand-dipped Belgian truffles the hotel put out for turndown service. But Joshua was prepared. He was a concierge. He was always prepared.

Lauren peered through the door. "You can't be serious."

"Why not?" Joshua paused his wiping the condensation off the slender, colorful cans. "It's not the strangest request we've had this week."

"No, that would be finding a salon to dye the Chinese Crested half-bald rat-dog lavender to match 4502's outfit for the wedding." Lauren had had a few choice words to say about the matching purple bitches—both of them seemed inclined to nip.

"It's kind of cool to be asked for something completely new. We ought to be able to fulfill this, really." Joshua wanted desperately to fulfill both Craig Ridley's wishes and his own. A couple of hours together. As friends. Maybe more. *Yeah, in your dreams, Joshua. Stay professional.*

"Don't see how we could organize staff for it if such a thing only comes up once in a blue moon," Lauren observed.

"Well, we don't have staff now, so I'm just going to take care of it myself." Joshua'd arm-wrestle anyone else for the privilege if they'd had such specialized staff. He tucked the fruit sodas and cards into a Barney's bag left over from meeting some guest's whim, before Lauren or anyone else could crush his plans.

"Don't you think you should find out a little more about this guy before you waltz into the best sound-proofed suite in New York City at the midnight hour?" she pointed out. "When I'm the only one who knows where you are, and I'm going home?"

"When you put it that way…" Joshua stopped in his tracks, heart jolting in his chest. An image flashed through his mind of the guy in the penthouse in a face mask, swinging a meat cleaver. Damn. He'd watched too many horror movies as a kid. However, he could winkle all kinds of secrets out of the Internet. He dove into the most recent entries. "Hmm. Nothing horrible coming up. No crimes…"

"That you know of," Lauren observed over his shoulder. "Not everything hits the news."

"Money doesn't hide everything." The man had enough money to hide a lot of things, even before the deal that brought him to New York this time. The society snippets didn't mention a wife… "If he's a total shitstain, I bail. I can survive an hour or two of whatever he doles out, I think. The worst he can do is bore me."

Joshua didn't expect to be bored.

"And the best he can do is jump your bones?"

That was the problem with concierges—the perception that made Lauren good at her job was also what made her an intermittent pain in the ass. Of course the best thing would be… Except for it being a fast track to the end of his career. Joshua wouldn't make that kind of sacrifice for a casual lay, and as for going Henry's route, fuck no. Even if it would get him unquestioned time alone with this particular guest. "That's not what he wants, Lauren, or he would have let you turn him over to Henry. I'm company. And I'm not looking to get fired." Joshua refrained from sticking his tongue out at her only because the general manager was speaking with Henry and didn't need to see Joshua acting unprofessional.

Maybe he could escape before Grant came to chat with the concierges. Joshua didn't want to detail the days' requests, nor tally the revenue. He'd keep his extra cigars until he needed a bigger bribe than he did right now.

"I still think it's nuts." Lauren scrolled down a page of Wall Street Journal links, trade site links, and a Wikipedia page.

Joshua clicked the browser shut. "Look, did we, or did we not find a matched pair of tame ocelots for the Hilton party?"

"We did," she agreed, digging her purse out of the drawer.

"So, if we can manage that, a little thing like rent-a-friend ought not to defeat us. It's a matter of pride, don't you think?" With that, Joshua waved at their oncoming relief. Nick could take over and worry about whatever middle of the night desires the rest of the hotel might develop.

His one remaining task of the night, to spend some innocent time with an interesting guy. No reason for his heart to speed up, not for business. The warm prickles on the back of his neck had to be the cool kiss of the lobby's ventilation, not anticipation. He studied his blurry reflection in the brass elevator doors. Did he still look as put together and crisp as he had this morning? He had to do his hotel proud. Only that. Right?

Joshua let the elevator doors close on him before he let himself grin at what else his Google-fu turned up. There was a woman named Felicity in Craig Ridley's life—as an employee.

Chapter Five

The rap at the door slightly after eleven jerked Craig away from the e-book he was reading with indifferent attention; if this was a thriller, he wasn't nearly as thrilled by the text as he was by the interruption.

Perhaps he should have peeked through the peephole, but anyone who knocked on this door had to use the passcard in the elevator, soooo… He opened the door.

Very scenic.

The vision he'd seen coming out of the suite earlier greeted him. Brown eyes under full brows, a perfectly straight nose over a sunny smile, wide shoulders dressed in a decent suit—the same label as the one Craig had treated himself to when he'd sold his first company.

He jerked his gaze back to his visitor's face—a laser dissection of the visitor's charms was just not okay. Not when Craig made it abundantly clear he wanted nothing but company. The guy was worth looking at—and an unknown quantity as to what kind of person he'd prove to be.

Ten seconds of admiration for the view. Would this stranger last longer once words started coming out of his mouth?

"I'm Joshua Hannes. You rang?" The smile faltered for a scant second.

Craig found his voice and the memory of why he needed it. "I'm Craig Ridley." Oh, that was stupid, of course rent-a-friend would know that, but... "Didn't I see you earlier?"

"You did—I arranged your dinner. Now I'm back. If that's okay." Joshua remained in the doorway, a bag dangling from his fingertips.

Oh, right, Craig was keeping him standing. He ushered his guest in. "Hope you brought the Scrabble board, or that there's one tucked away in some yet to be explored corner here."

"I don't think so, but I found us a deck of cards. We could play gin rummy, or War, or Go Fish." Joshua pulled the sealed deck from his bag.

"Definitely more social than watching a movie." Craig slit the cellophane wrapper to shake out the cards. "Or we could talk politics and possibly have our first fight, or compare weight lifting routines if we both lifted... Sorry, I didn't even think about going downstairs to the gym to burn off some energy—I'm exhausted but my body still swears it's two hours too early to go to bed."

"No problem." His visitor's smile looked genuine. "I brought some Izzes." He found coasters in the sideboard inlaid with enough exotic woods to endanger an entire rainforest, and two cut crystal tumblers, which he filled with ice from a minifridge disguised as more finely milled cabinetry. "Pomegranate, blackberry, or peach?"

Craig studied a maroon can, searching for symbols. Packaging had betrayed him before. "Is this kosher?"

Joshua examined his own can. "I don't think it's certified, but it's vegan. Is that close enough?"

"Sure is. Blackberry sounds good." He poured and offered to clink his glass against Joshua's peach drink. "To new friends."

Josh gave him *that* look again, a nanosecond of *I don't understand*. "*L'chaim?*"

"La kayim," Craig agreed. Whatever that meant. Probably New-Yorkese. That gravelly consonant might just be another regional thing. Craig sipped again, the fruity bubbles dancing on his tongue.

Nice choice—Craig could appreciate the subtlety of not bringing wine or liquor. This wasn't a date. What the hell did they do next? Cards, okay—another nice choice. Joshua hadn't mentioned poker. Not when that could go lascivious. Not that Craig would mind in the least demanding shirts and trousers as forfeit.

Stop. That. One more stray thought and he'd have to adjust himself. The thin sweats he'd changed into for lounging wouldn't hide a thing. Besides, where the hell had that thought come from? That was twice now. His interest hadn't been piqued like this in years.

"So, gin rummy?" Craig offered.

"You're on." Joshua produced a pad and pen from a work of art generally shaped like a desk.

They sorted out their versions of the rules into mutual agreement, and Craig dealt out the cards. "We need some stakes."

"Money?" Joshua stilled. "Or…?"

Damn it—even the small things worked against this rent-a-friend business. That "or" had to be exactly why his companion hadn't mentioned poker. He hadn't removed his suit coat, only pulling the knot of his tie away from his throat and undoing the top button.

Craig liked the lack of assumptions. What else could he like about Joshua? "Lose a round, answer a question, is that okay?" Damn it, that could go bad again fast— Joshua stopped sorting his hand. "Getting to know you kind of questions, nothing super-personal."

"That works." Joshua relaxed again. "Prepare to lose."

"You can try," Craig shot back, and took the top card from the stack.

They picked and discarded, traded jibes about their hands, and snapped the cards down on the table. "Gin!" Joshua declared over a fan of runs and groups.

"Whoa, sixty-five points and a question to the loser." Craig totted up the mess in his hand and braced himself. "What would you like to know?"

"Did you like the elephant?"

"Yeah, I did. Both of them." Craig liked the question. "Is that something you do a lot?"

"Never. It's more of a cruise thing, I think. If I'd had more time to practice, I would have done the dog. It was cute." Joshua dealt out the cards. "Too complicated for a first try."

"Okay, maybe a dog by Friday? For a man who needs a best friend?" Damn that sounded needy once it was out of his mouth. Craig refused to flinch.

"I'm never going to look at a towel the same again." Joshua sorted his cards and the competition was on.

"Gin." Craig parlayed a good starting hand into a quick victory. "Hockey or football?"

That took Joshua aback. "Neither," he said after a moment's pondering. "If I'm going to watch something, it would be skiing, or skating. Hockey's just a problem to be solved for me, like can I get six rink-side tickets to a Rangers game. Football is all about 'how early do I need to order cars to get out to the stadium?'"

"So, if you were at a Super Bowl party, you'd be the one making nachos?" Craig asked.

"Probably, but I'd watch large men falling on each other in public."

Joshua buried that statement in a flurry of shuffling. Craig liked the pinkness growing in his cheeks, but wouldn't stare. Too openly. "That's the best part of football."

Oh damn, there he went, overstepping a boundary. Maybe.

Maybe not. Craig collected a fistful of queens and aces, winning again. He kept his questions innocuous, but liking what he learned about Joshua. Hoping Joshua found him interesting. Keeping the questions to "Harry Potter or Game of Thrones?" level still told him a lot about the man, every bit of it enticing. Joshua could get right through his barricades and never know it.

Was he getting as much out of Craig's answers to "what's your favorite movie?" or "bleu cheese, yes or no?" Each bit of conversation let slip more than Craig intended, and told him more than perhaps Joshua meant for him to know for even asking.

The cards fell Craig's way again, in long runs of hearts. "What do you like about being a concierge?"

Joshua leaned back in his seat, pondering. "Part of it's pleasing the client. Doing something that makes them happy, or that they need. Part of it's the challenge. It's not really that I want people playing 'stump the concierge', but accomplishing something I hadn't imagined before. People tend to be relatively consistent in their desires, so a new request is fun."

So was looking at the satisfaction on his face. Craig clung to staff who looked that pleased with their jobs. Damn few to cling to, really.

His competitive streak also had a question. "So, was the rent-a-friend request something ordinary or new?"

"New, absolutely." Joshua had relaxed enough to cross his ankle over his knee.

The view was mostly hidden by the table. Craig forced himself not to try looking at the apex of those muscular thighs. How could he go from zero to want in one evening? Probably a good thing he was starting to droop—that lessened the possibility of saying something to tense Joshua up again.

"I mean, people want tour guides, or massages, or some kind of personal service on a daily basis." The next thought put both of his feet on the ground. "Or sex. Which we don't provide. But companionship? That's new."

Well, at least Craig had done something memorable. "I'm asking to know, not asking to get. But you seem really jumpy about the whole issue, and everyone keeps bringing up sex, when I haven't. Is that a hotel thing, or a New York thing, or what?"

Joshua shook his head, dark locks fluttering over his forehead. "A hotel issue. The obvious, of course, it's not legal, the hotel doesn't want the reputation or the hassle, yada, yada, yada. Then there's the fraud aspect—my department's eaten the cost on more than a few pairs of Jimmy Choos. Maybe they were regrettable gifts, maybe the escort was taking advantage while the client was in the bathroom. We concierges have a lot of responsibility. When you have access to someone's double-titanium credit card, you have to keep things under control."

Craig hadn't even imagined such things. "Maybe I'm sheltered. But your colleague did offer a referral. Seems... odd?"

Joshua was gonna rumple his eyebrows the way he rubbed his palm over his face like that. "Lauren's usually more discreet. I think you rattled her. But this is New York, and the Vivaldi is full of rich people, so if you want two exotics and a Viagra, someone will supply. Just don't ask me."

"I won't. Yeesh." Craig couldn't imagine wanting such a situation—what would they talk about after they got out of bed? Or before? Craig was starting to feel the need to get into a bed—a yawn threatened to blossom. But he didn't want to turn loose of this unexpectedly fascinating man just yet. "You want to play another hand, or just ask a question?"

Joshua gathered the cards into a tidy pile and stuffed them back into the box. "What does SecurNow actually do?"

Craig offered the quick version. "We do data security for cloud-based applications, HIPAA-compliant level. Healthcare and insurance mostly, but we're moving into the financial sector too. There's a lot of threat out there. Do you want details?"

A yawn hit Joshua hard enough Craig could feel the pop of his jaw. "I'm not sure I could understand the tech parts."

Yawns were contagious—Craig had to cover his mouth and wait it out. "Take it as a given, our services are in great demand. We're plowing most of the IPO money into expansion."

"How did you get into something like that? It sounds terribly techie and necessary to modern web-based commerce." Joshua sounded genuinely interested.

Okay, Crain would tell him the sad story. "In my case, because I couldn't do what I really wanted to do anymore. The perils of selling out. My first company was something I started while I was still in college, a fee-accessed compendium of old texts, meant to augment, or replace, all the expensive books I was getting gouged for."

Joshua groaned. "Been there. Shared books with class-mates and waited on line for the reserve copies. Bet you were popular."

Maybe anyone willing to deface a necessary book as hard as Craig had would have been as popular—and done more to capitalize on it. Saturday nights for Craig were free evenings to slice off bindings and scan. "Oh, I was. Trigonometry hasn't changed much in the last hundred and fifty years, or translations of Plato and Euripides. Anything but science, that changes too fast for public domain to keep up. Marketed it to my classmates and started offering it on other campuses. I was making some bank on it. Might have been the first in my class to make my first million."

However many millions Craig Ridley might have made since, that first must have come from his passion. Joshua watched the emotions chase the memories in Craig's face, and listened raptly to his story with barely an "uh huh" or "mm." Nope, no chance of the guy boring him.

"This did not go unnoticed by the campus bookstore, so they waved cash at me, said I could stay on, with salary and bonuses, get some help running it. Too good to be true, you know?" He glanced at Joshua with a wry quirk of his mouth.

Joshua could sympathize. "What happened?"

"Should have read the non-compete agreement better. I was out on my ass before you could say 'second edition'." Craig laughed ruefully. "They shut that puppy down and might have raised the price of every textbook in the store a buck for revenge. I'd agreed to stay out of that field for fifteen years, should I leave the company. For any reason."

"Damn." Joshua would have run, waving what little money he'd had then, to sign up for Craig's service. "What happens after fifteen years?"

"We shall see," Craig rumbled. "Soon. I have a few ideas."

Plus fifteen-years' better tech and a grudge? And the drive to go from scrounging to the Central Park Suite? That bookstore was in for it now. "I bet you have lots of ideas."

"Plenty." Craig sipped the last dribbles of his fruit drink. "I used a few of them and the bookstore money to start Quatnatics. We got a couple products to market, hadn't turned a profit yet, but we were poised to, and then Google bought us. If you've used Nymfi you've used Quatnatics' stuff."

"All the time. Wow." Man, did it make his life easier. And this guy created it? Falling at Craig's feet out of gratitude was liable to be misconstrued. Or not. Admiration mixed with lust could result in unmistakable BJs. "But you moved on?"

"Yup. Wasn't interested in being a cog in the corporate environment. I'd rather run the corporation, make the decisions. Going public is going to mess with my control some, but give us some better opportunities than if we financed our growth with borrowing. Always a trade-off, you know?" He spoke over his shoulder, while clearing their glasses to the counter by the miniature sink. "I think we do some good in the world."

Not a word about making shitloads of money. Even if he was rolling in folding green, or would be after the IPO. Not a word about the big-boy toys. He wasn't even wearing a Rolex or a Breitling. Whatever was important to this man mattered a whole lot more than the money.

Craig yawned. "Dang, I'm glad someone else is minding the store tonight. Time for bed."

Joshua's heart skipped a beat. The man didn't mean… *Play, it cool, man, play it cool!* If he was making suggestions he'll have to work a lot harder. Calling on years of professionalism, Joshua forced all emotion from his face and voice. This wasn't an invitation. It couldn't be. "I'll be on my way then. This city may never sleep, but I need to." He rubbed his face again. "At least I get to sleep late tom—Oh shit. No, I don't."

★ ★ ★ ★ ★

"What did you forget?" Craig remembered sleeping late. Once. Two companies ago.

"I traded shifts with Deb." Joshua stood up fast enough to half-knock his chair over—he caught it before it fell. "Damn it. I'll have to grab a cab. At least it's faster than the subway."

"What time do you have to be in?" What was the guy's problem?

"Eight. Up at six. With all the construction around town, rush hour's going to be hideous. The trains will be double squished." Joshua slapped his pockets.

Oh, that. Craig had lucked into more hotel than he could possibly use. Why not share the wealth? Wasn't like Joshua didn't know about the king-sized bed. "Tomorrow's going to be fine. You're sleeping here."

This Craig guy was good company—there had to be a reason he was renting a friend instead of being surrounded by them. Maybe just being a stranger in the city? Once the initial weirdness wore off, they'd gotten along just fine, and it wasn't like he'd put any kind of move on. That's how it got to be well after one a.m. before Joshua even noticed. Half an hour to his bed still, and the morning didn't bear thinking about. Three and a half hours of sleep if he was lucky. "This was fun but I need to go, or tomorrow's going to suck."

Mr. I'm-Wired-So-Come-Keep-Me-Company didn't seem too bothered by that, and why should he? Didn't mean he should be all nonchalant and tell Joshua where he should sleep. Hadn't the whole point of tonight been *not* sleeping here?

After all the effort he'd put into keeping the situation low-key, and then outright explaining, Craig went and said *that*.

"Um, no, don't think so." Joshua took a step back and patted his pockets. Yeah, had his keys. A can of pepper spray, too, but that was a last resort. "I'll be fine. Good times, don't say it hasn't been…" He sidled around the table, keeping Craig firmly in his sights.

"Try not to be stupid, of course you're staying here." Craig stood between him and the door. "You can get a couple more hours of sleep, and your day will go all the better."

Joshua's pulse pounded in his ears. How had things gone south so fast? Stupid, stupid, stupid! Of course the guy wanted more than conversation, and likely saw Joshua's sticking around as interest. Which it was. But not happening. Keeping his voice as firm and level as possible, he ground out, "Didn't I make it clear?" Should he go through Craig, or dodge around? Or just throw himself into the man's arms? "I'm not sleeping with you."

"Didn't say you were." Craig tapped a finger against his own forehead. "Think."

Joshua was too tired to think, and the aftermath from these shenanigans wouldn't improve that. But that was scorn in Craig's voice, not invitation, which halted Joshua halfway to the door. "What?"

Marching across the plush carpet, Craig motioned a *come on*. "Friends don't make friends go home in the dark."

He swung open the door, making a grand "after you" gesture. It wasn't the master bedroom. "There's two bedrooms—this one's yours. If you're smart enough to take it." Nothing in the man's casual manner suggested deception.

Could he be making an honest, innocent suggestion?

If so, foot, meet mouth. "Uh, thank you." Stay? Or go? A trim, lightly muscled man in a T and sweats waving him through a doorway ought to be following him right to the bed. Joshua hated coming closer with no way to come as close as he wanted. Somehow, knowing sex was off the table made him want it even more. "Sorry, I shouldn't have assumed...."

Craig patted his shoulder, patting him right through the door. "Damned right you shouldn't." Just before he swung the door completely shut, Craig said, "Wait to be asked."

Wait to be asked? The words slammed ice into Joshua's belly. Sure didn't sound like there'd be any asking, ever.

Well, hell. How to look like complete jerk in one easy step. Craig could have let him leave, with a cheery wave and an "It's been fun," and let Joshua stumble through tomorrow. Erm, today. Instead, he'd offered the difference between hell and okay. Guess if Joshua hadn't had tunnel vision on what an overnight stay meant, he could have been a whole lot more gracious about being put up in the lap of luxury.

He'd have to find a way to apologize properly. Still, his head reeled. No one offered something for nothing.

He strained to listen, breathing a sigh of relief—or was it frustration?—when the door on the other side of the suite clicked shut.

So, an honest to goodness, no strings attached favor.

Which traded one set of problems for another.

His suit would do for a second day, and his shirt...

A white shirt was a white shirt, shouldn't be a mark of shame. Joshua hung everything up to air in a closet slightly larger than his share of the apartment he wasn't sleeping in tonight. The tie, though…

He could liberate something from the lost and found. Enough ties got left behind in the hotel's bars that he should be able to find something to his taste. Or at least not sporting Scotch stains.

No way around a second day in these boxers, though several hours' airing would help. He could lock the door, although the sting of *Wait to be asked* was more secure than any deadbolt from Schlage or Chubb. Couldn't keep a man from dreaming, though.

All the amenities the hotel set out as a matter of course for guests came to his rescue now—toothbrush, toothpaste, a miniature deodorant for the morning. He fell into bed, nude against the soft, thousand-thread-count sheets, only to find his conscience was too lumpy to sleep on.

He should go apologize right now. He should stay the hell out of the master bedroom, where Craig was peeling off those thin sweatpants and climbing into bed alone.

Alone was not how Joshua wanted this night, no matter what came out of his mouth. Self-preservation and what he wanted didn't match up nearly as often as they should.

He'd been told to wait until he was asked, and Craig hadn't asked him for a thing. Had put him in the second bedroom, like he'd never ask.

This was all kinds of fucked up, saying no when he meant *yes, please, take me.*

If Craig had asked, would Joshua have answered with his self-preservation or his desires?

Joshua's cock knew what it wanted. Who it wanted. Hard and full against his belly. Every throb told Joshua to pad across the plush carpet to the other bedroom and ask humbly to join Craig in his king-sized bed.

Joshua wrapped his hand around his erection with a small sob of frustration. Here he was, here he'd stay until morning. Alone. But he could dream of Craig taking him in hand, wrapping those well-manicured fingers around Joshua's stiff dick. Jacking him slowly, letting him feel the anticipation and the slide of skin over core.

Raising his spread knees lifted the sheets away from his chest and gave the Craig in his head a place to kneel. A view of Joshua's private places, a glimpse of the rosy pucker where Joshua wanted a finger, or two. Or more—did he dare dream of Craig sliding his cock inside?

Joshua wrapped his other hand around his balls, rolling the delicate ovals under the skin. Craig would cradle his nuts while jacking him. That brilliant smile would praise him for succumbing to the pleasure of Craig's touch...

His imagination took him farther over the edge than his hands did—he spurted over his own skin, pulsing against his palms. His climax shook him from prostate on out, forcing another whimper through his clenched jaws. His thighs quivered from the intensity. The hours he'd spent with Craig were foreplay. They took their toll on him now.

Great, he'd made a mess. The towel elephant lay toppled and unrolling next to Joshua—he shook the head back into a hand towel to wipe up his splatters before they dripped to the sheets.

If touching himself was this good, what would it be like with the real Craig between his knees?

He'd never find out.

Joshua rolled against the down pillows and hoped for a visitor in the night.

Craig specialized in solutions to problems that had to be fixed before they happened. Fixing Joshua's problem was easy enough, and like any easy fix, it spawned three more problems.

Shutting the door on Joshua didn't begin to shut the door on Craig's thoughts. He'd put a hunk of lumber between himself and temptation, and it wasn't doing him a lick of good.

Even doing the rent-a-friend thing might be a problem for Joshua—was he on the clock? Or not? Or—the last thing Craig wanted was for his lovely evening with a fascinating man to be a paid obligation.

Why did he have to meet this delectable person by phoning the concierge desk for a rent-a-friend?

Had it fucked up any chance they had for something more? Wait—he was really thinking about something more after a couple of hours? Desire was so unfamiliar as to be nearly unrecognizable. When was the last time he'd even wanted…? But Craig definitely wanted Joshua.

Joshua lay behind two doors and so many misgivings. Sleep might be eluding him as much as it eluded Craig. He sent a squashy down pillow flying across the room out of sheer frustration for its pliability. Not the elephant. The terry critter could stay—Joshua made him. He was a little bit of Joshua's personality in Craig's bed. Its towel flesh gave softly when Craig squeezed it.

He could go knock. Say, "I'm sorry, I shouldn't have snapped. Invite me in?"

Right. When the whole problem was Joshua turning him down before he'd even asked.

The clock ticked off another half hour and Craig hadn't come any closer to sleep. The bedside table might contain an answer.

He fumbled the Aneros out of its velvet pouch and found the lube. What would Joshua think of his toy? Did he use something similar? Would he want to try? Or would he be freaked out by the ecstasy Craig could bring for himself with nothing but a toy and practice?

Slipping the prostate stimulator into place, Craig wished it were Joshua's fingers. He settled the toy just so, turning to his side to let it find the sweet spot. Had he the time, and was less frantic about the man who lay so near and yet out of reach, he'd clench himself into a no-hands climax that would rattle his bones.

Tonight he wanted hands, hands that weren't his own. Hands he'd have to eat a big portion of crow to be touched by. He needed to feel those hands on his cock, to dream that Joshua was finding out his sensitive places and all the things that made him melt, or cry out, or come.

He'd never given a rat's ass about the beautiful men who threw themselves at him daily, because nothing he wished to hear came out of their mouths. He wanted reality, he wanted personality, he didn't need flattery or thinly veiled greed. He wanted more of what he'd had tonight, of all the good things Joshua had given him. Dinner, talk, space, interest. No pressure. The opposite of pressure. Company.

He made do with his hand on his erection, stroking the thick column and thumbing the edge of the fat head. He clenched his ass on the toy, pressing it into the sweet spot like a lover's finger. Pressing his face into the pillow, he muffled his hoarse call. It wasn't Joshua's shoulder, much as he wished to stifle his noises against soft skin. Did Joshua manscape? Or was he natural, rough here and there with hair?

He might never know for sure, the way he might never know if Joshua would take Craig's cock deep into his mouth and lave him for the shared joy of playing.

The jets of semen he shot spattered into the elephant's absorbent folds. Joshua's elephant.

It should have been Joshua's mouth.

Chapter Six

The opening and closing of the suite's front door and soft voices woke Joshua. Damn, how early did Craig get up?

Joshua sped through the shower, grateful for the fluffy towels and complimentary toiletries. The razor was disposable, but a high-grade Schick Quattro, as good as his razor at home. He wiped the last of the suds and beard away and wrapped himself in the rest of the elephant to answer the knock on his bedroom door.

"Good morning," Craig said, a high-end department store bag dangling from his fingertips.

"Wow. Thanks." Joshua had trouble tearing his eyes away from the vision of Craig, his shirt open and his tie yet untied but draped around his neck. His hair was still damp and curling at the ends.

Maybe the double wrap of heavy terrycloth would keep Joshua's dick under control.

"I figured you might need these." Craig handed over the bag.

Joshua pulled not one but two shirts out, and a length of burgundy silk speckled with tiny dragonflies.

"I guessed on your shirt size, but a 15 ½, 34/35 should work, right?"

"Good guess," Joshua said weakly. "Why two?"

"In case there's a future need. Rent-a-friends work some crazy hours." Craig buttoned his shirt while Joshua gaped at the unexpected gift. "Don't worry about it. I figured you might not want to go to work in the entirely same outfit as yesterday."

"Um, well, no." If it was doubtful, it was dirty, and Joshua hadn't liked the whiff of his shirt last night. "'Where' is Barney's, obviously, but how?"

"Equally obviously, I called the concierge desk and told them what I wanted, and when I needed it. Your colleague Nick was quite prompt." Craig grinned at his own cleverness. "See, I am learning."

Craig obviously had the hang of how, but he'd missed some nuances.

"Um, this is to keep me from doing a walk of shame, right?" Joshua stared at the Perry Ellis tie, wanting Craig to tie the knot under his chin.

Craig nodded, his trousers open so he could tuck his shirt tails in. Only for shirt tails. Please let him not be teasing.

"Then I can't wear this." Even though the tiny dragonflies blended into an abstract pattern until you looked closely, and Joshua might have chosen it for himself.

Craig quirked an eyebrow. "Why not?"

"If Nick brought it, he's seen it. He knows where it went, and I can't come downstairs to take over without him drawing some conclusions. You know what he'd think." Nick wouldn't hesitate to share his conclusions, either—he'd been desperate to move to a day shift for the last year and a half. "I should probably wear the blue from yesterday. The fresh shirt will make it all fine."

"Oh, well, if that's the only problem." Craig plucked the dragonfly tie from Joshua's unresisting fingers. "I'll wear it. Let him think I lost a suitcase or that the hick from Denver didn't bring proper business attire with him. No skin off my nose."

"True," Joshua agreed, ready to punch Nick over the "hick" designation, until he recalled whose words they were.

"And you wear this." Craig pulled the bright magenta silk, patterned in subtle dots of white and teal, from his own neck, and hung it over Joshua's shoulder. "That ought to be eye-searing enough to keep anyone from looking at your suit too closely."

"Not even out of my usual style, either." Joshua had an array of bright neckwear, from vintage Gucci bees to hand-painted silk older than his father. "Thanks."

"I wasn't sure what to do about breakfast, though. Should I have room service bring something up?" Craig, mostly organized now and wrapping the dragonfly tie into a tidy knot by touch, sounded worried. "I'm presuming already."

Craig had already done more than Joshua was comfortable with. "No, this is great. I'll grab something from the kitchen downstairs before I go on. Unless you're hungry?"

"Morgenthau Pierce will have a bagel spread or some such—we still have a lot to do." Craig looked nearly ready to go, and Joshua had better get a move on—the slender timepiece on Craig's wrist showed half an hour to showtime.

"Do you have transport? Do you need transport?"

Joshua kicked into professional mode even though his hair still dripped.

"I'll have the doorman catch me a cab. I hear they're wild little bucksnorters." Craig grinned. "I may even survive the ride."

That answered the Rolls Royce question. Badly. "I have a better idea." He ducked back into his room and found his phone, with enough charge left to fix this issue. "Salvator, *buenos días*. Our gentleman in the Central Park Suite needs to get to Wall Street this fine morning. How long before you can be at the front door? *Bueno, bueno!*" He hung up, grinning, until his towel started to slip. He grabbed the waistline and managed to halt the slide. After last night, that would be either disastrous or ridiculous.

"Ah, what am I looking for?" Craig looked dubious. Maybe because he didn't get a show?

"A Flying Lady on the bonnet of a black Rolls Royce Silver Wraith, in fifteen minutes. Comes with the suite." Joshua winked. "I have the world's shortest commute this morning, you have the world's most comfortable. There should be a Wall Street Journal outside, if you hadn't already brought it in."

"I found it." Craig chuckled, shaking his head. "A Rolls Royce. For me. Unreal. Go get dressed. Leave your stuff here, don't want to blow your cover." He shooed Joshua back into the room.

While Joshua pressed the package wrinkles out of his shirt, he allowed himself to believe Craig kept him standing in a towel toga because he liked the view.

There wouldn't be any goodbye kisses for this leave-taking. Joshua stood next to Craig in the elevator, cautious about mentioning anything personal, while they collected other passengers from floors 52 through 26. Butter wouldn't melt in Craig's mouth from the looks of it—he stared straight ahead as if Joshua was a stranger.

Which, yeah, he was. Kind of. But it was protection too, because no one in the hotel needed to know he'd spent the night in a guest's room. No matter what they had or hadn't done.

When the elevator decanted them in the hushed marble lobby and the half dozen suits with briefcases marched on without them, Craig hung back a few steps. Not knowing what else to do, Joshua slowed with him, all the way to a stop.

"Ah, I'll be letting the concierge desk know about dinner plans," Craig said, not making eye contact with Joshua. "Probably around eight again. You're probably off earlier than yesterday too."

"I am," Joshua replied, not knowing where to take this. "Let me know what you'd like for dinner, okay?"

The words weren't half out of his mouth when it struck him how old-married-couple that sounded. With a man he hadn't kissed, and probably never would. But it brought a smile to Craig's face. "I will."

That smile brought Joshua a good four inches off the floor on his trip to the kitchen. He even saluted the housekeeper rubbing a gleam into the bronze hand rails in the back hallway. Who cared if Amaya didn't smile back?

He dashed through the kitchen to snag a quick egg biscuit before the platter got carried out to the buffet. Full of breakfast and hope and wearing a $300 tie—that he'd need to return—life looked pretty darn good. Time to fulfill requests, make people happy. Those high-end restaurants and symphony seats weren't going to fill themselves.

He had the desk to himself this morning, normally a slack time anyway. He still managed to acquire a half dozen tips paid in Franklins, for knowing when Christie's had both a Chagall and a Picasso in an upcoming auction, making dinner reservations for four at Masa, and arranging a private fitting at a famous designer's salon. He sent two guests out for a scenic ride around Central Park on the hotel's bicycles, with directions to stop at the Strawberry Fields memorial and not to feed the geese. Bring it on, even if a debutante threw a small fit for not being able to adopt a chi-wienie that very afternoon, because they were so cute before their eyes opened! He'd found three litters of chi-wienies, hadn't he? Couldn't she let the little beasts grow up a bit?

Patience wasn't the strong suit of anyone who called the Vivaldi's concierge desk, but Joshua had reservations, tickets, appointments, tchotchkes, and necessities sent to this one and that one, and by the time Lauren and Deb showed up, he had everything under control. The incoming calls would create havoc, but that would be Lauren and Deb's problem for a bit. "Taking a break, guys," he called over his shoulder. Had to dash before Lauren started asking questions.

He turned up in the kitchen just in time to intercept a plate of shrimp scampi, sent back by some overpampered idiot for the dish containing garlic. The diner clearly had no idea what to expect and was throwing their weight around because they could. Their loss, Joshua's gain. His friendship with the *commis* and the expediter paid off every time, if he wasn't picky, and with food like this, who would be? Plus, his good timing left him a few minutes to run upstairs.

Because no matter what their relationship started as, Joshua wanted Craig to know he was damned good at what he did. And that he wasn't always a prickly little shit.

Plus, a guy who slaved away in the salt mines needed a little pick-me-up.

Joshua let himself into the suite he'd left scarcely six hours earlier, entering to the sound of the vacuum cleaner and the lemon fumes of furniture polish. Not a problem—as far as anyone knew, he was here on official business. Which he was. Kind of.

All the same, he headed to the bedroom farthest from the sound of the vacuum, the one he'd slept in last night. All made up and pristine, as if no one had ever crawled under the covers and whacked off. At least he'd rinsed his cum-rag this morning. He snagged the freshly hung towels and proceeded to botch a kitty on his first try. He flipped the towel out and started over.

In his concentration, he didn't notice the silence descend. He did notice the sharp, "Hey! *Pato*! You wrecking my hard work again?"

Damn but he wished he hadn't levitated at the sound of Paolina's voice. Twice his age and with eyes that had seen things, she managed to scare him in spite of himself. She had a grudge, she didn't have power, but that didn't keep him from needing to shake out his dignity like a cloak before answering.

"I'm performing a service a guest requested, thank you very much." He gave her the barest of courtesy before turning back to his creation.

"Some service, messing up hard work. That's what you do." She wouldn't spit on the floor she'd left immaculate, but she might as well have for all the contempt she flung.

"I said I was sorry." Joshua had split the tip for the lube party with her and Amaya, netting them close to an additional week's take home pay, under the table. If she didn't want to let bygones be bygones, there wasn't much else he could do.

"Some service," she repeated. "What other kinds of service you give this guest? Ah?"

How did this harridan in a polyester apron manage such venom?

"Dinner and a deck of cards, nothing unusual." Fold double, roll the edges, ignore Paolina…

"Sure, sure," she scoffed. "Maybe service on your knees, *pato?* "

"It's a good thing your rooms aren't as filthy as your mind," Joshua snapped. "And quit calling me a duck."

She laughed, a thick ugly sound. "Of course, little duck. Call *me* filthy?" She turned across the thick carpet in her sensible, thick-soled fashion disasters, wheeling her cart out the door. "You don't want to be *pato?* Okay, you can be *puto.*"

He understood the malice in that term well enough, and maybe now the other, something his textbook Spanish hadn't addressed. Still, she had nothing but bitterness, and it was wearing on him. Could he call in enough favors to get this woman a job at the Marcel?

An annoyed Deb handed Joshua the phone like he was taking money out of her pocket. "He asked for you by name."

Yes! It was Craig! "Order from Mikeleh's again tonight. We should be done early enough to plan for dinner at eight. Something lamb. You're off at five?"

Grateful for Craig's phrasing and wary of the other two concierges, Joshua confirmed the time.

"Oh, well. Um." Craig didn't go past that. "You did have a long day yesterday…"

There was absolutely nothing Craig could add to that without a dead giveaway and a couple of assumptions. "Lamb at eight, no problem."

Yeah, that was a problem, and maybe all in his own mind.

If it was a problem, Joshua was going to fix it. He sped out the gleaming glass doors at 5:01, past an astonished Henry and the doorman. Home first, a crowded subway ride to the East Village, where he ignored his roommate's questions and slipped out of his blue suit.

Best thing about this apartment—closet space. Okay, and a bed, but mostly the closet space. His wardrobe lived here more than he did. Too many other things to do, places to be, to spend a bigger chunk of his income on an apartment of his own. Maybe if he met someone, it would be time to look.

Might be possible to find something bigger than 500 square feet in a neighborhood he liked for under a million bucks.

The 50 percent down payment would cut his reserves a tad thin. Maybe he should add this week's tips to the real estate fund.

Nah. Maybe he'd buy stock of Craig's company instead. The folding green would buy three or four hundred shares. Let them grow, and he could get another 100 square feet of apartment. When there was a need.

Joshua debated the gray pinstripe versus jeans and a sweater, but the suit would look fine for his purposes. He'd blend in, and maybe it would be a subtle hint.

Then across town, to a toy store, and then uptown towards Mikeleh's. He collected a lamb shank, fragrant with rosemary, and requested a second on his own credit card. The four short blocks to the Vivaldi was a quick walk even with his burdens.

He made it to the hotel at a quarter of eight, in time to see the gleaming black Rolls Royce pull up under the porte cochère. The doorman opened the rear door for Craig and received a discreet handshake for his trouble. Good to see Craig knew the drill—had he thanked Salvator correctly?

Best to nip through the side door, lest he have to run the gauntlet of Deb and Lauren, or explain to Henry that no, he was not taking anything at all up to the penthouse suite. Joshua came at the banks of elevators from the back unaccosted and slipped his pilfered keycard into the penthouse slot.

Five minutes to eight, perfect. Joshua knocked two quick raps on the door. Craig opened it, his eyes open wide as his smile over his loosened tie and open dress shirt.

"Lamb shanks at eight." Joshua grinned back. "I hear you like Scrabble."

"Why, yes, I do." Craig ushered him into the penthouse, where the lights of Manhattan twinkled through every window in a dark carpet of grounded stars. "But I don't like to eat alone. Shall I call room service?"

"No need." The suite had china and silver—he set the table from the contents of the elegant sideboard. "Since the Rent-a-friend dispenser was broken, you'll have to make do with me. I fetched for two."

Craig produced the recorked bottle of Rhone from the minifridge and poured into crystal goblets. "Perfect."

And it was.

Craig hadn't dared to hope that Joshua would stick around after a full day, just to bring dinner and a board game. But here he was, across a dining room table, looking like he belonged there. All good conversation—did the man know *everything* happening in this city? —mixed with exquisite food. With enough vocabulary and tactics to propel both their Scrabble scores well over two hundred.

If the Rent-a-friend dispenser only lasted long enough to emit Joshua, it had still exceeded its design specs.

The night wound down to the awkward point. "There's a towel kitty on your bed," Craig suggested. "The whiskers were a nice touch. I accidentally knocked the tail off mine when I sat down, but yours is perfect."

Joshua scooped tiles into the velvet bag and stowed the board back in the box. "Glad you liked it. They'd be sturdier if I stuck a few pins in, but that could be dangerous later."

Definitely could, if Joshua had used his elephant the same way Craig had. He could hope. He'd take the bull by the horns. It might even be a horny bull—Joshua wasn't wearing the same suit as this morning. "You're welcome to stay."

"I'd like to." Joshua's handsome face disappeared behind both hands, which didn't disguise the deep yawn. "Since I'm not a one-night-stand kind of guy."

"Good to know." Even if there wouldn't be so much as a goodnight kiss at the doorway. Even if he had to make do with his toys. He had enough time tonight for a proper hands-free session, especially with the fantasy fodder in the other bedroom.

"Might be time to call it a night. I need to be back on the desk at eight." Poor guy did look a bit bleary.

"There's another shirt in the closet," Craig reminded him. "Two shirts do not a kept man make."

"Keeping me isn't that easy." Joshua favored Craig with a steely glare.

"Okay." Craig would shoot that down now. "You can wear your own tie. It's still in the closet."

Why did mentioning the tie freeze him up?

Whatever the tie issue was, it didn't keep Joshua from disappearing behind a closed door. Well, might as well get his money's worth out of this luxurious suite. No sense in letting the bed go empty when it made Joshua's life easier.

Even if Craig was starting to wish Joshua had turned the other direction.

Because damn, he was the best company Craig could remember. Knowledgeable, pleasant company, willing to stand his ground, not pushy. Last night Craig would have bet on rent-a-friend turning into rent-a-dick, until Joshua made it so very plain he was having none of that.

Good. Or bad.

Because Joshua was starting to grow on him in a way that would be hard to give up. Craig's IPO launched on Friday, his plane left Saturday, and Joshua's life was here. His was in Denver.

All they had was now, and separate bedrooms.

A man could dream, and if the dreams came seldom, they had to be enjoyed twice as much. Craig pulled his toy out of its pouch and drizzled it with lube. Touching the tip to his hole, he pushed down to let the first bulb in. Like a finger, holding his ass open. He shouldn't be in a hurry, not when he could imagine Joshua being the one to penetrate him, slowly, gently, but firmly. With love and wanting. Might as well dream it all. He could dream of Joshua's cock filling him up with the next bump of the toy going in.

He turned, letting the toy settle, bringing the first familiar whispers of pleasure. Semi-flaccid, but it didn't matter—he'd learned to work his inner muscles as hard as his biceps. Craig tightened his pelvic floor, working the Aneros inside for some time that clocks didn't count—it might have been an hour or it might have been seven minutes—he didn't know and he didn't care. Not with the image of Joshua in a towel, still wet from the shower, dancing in his mind. He'd done well this morning to keep it cool, not lick the drips off Joshua's pecs or tug at the terrycloth to see it fall to the floor. To expose every inch of him.

Joshua might say no with his mouth, but his body said yes. He'd been at least semi-erect under that white towel, and he'd worked as hard as Craig had to keep his eyes up. Joshua wanted him. At least a little.

The toy danced over his gland with every contraction of his pelvic muscles, bringing the thrill of the prostate-waves. So much earlier than usual, but that was Joshua's doing, for being so beautifully half clad in Craig's mind, for being the kind of man he could talk to long enough to want physically.

Clutching the gift Joshua'd left, Craig pressed it to his groin. His first orgasm was dry, and his second, and third, nothing to catch. Could he teach Joshua this tantric pleasure—would he learn to enjoy a quiet, intense session? Craig would grease his ass, insert a toy and let him enjoy everything happening within while Craig stroked his skin and laid kisses everywhere. Then there'd be the down and dirty, because fuck the tantra when they were together in a bed and could indulge in the wildness of hard cocks in mouths and asses and bodies slapping together.

They'd mingle breaths and sweat and seed, and they'd fall back gasping into a pile where they didn't know which body was whose, or care.

He could dream, and he could come, in great splashes of wetness against the towel creature that wasn't a good substitute for the man who'd made it.

Chapter Seven

The long, gleaming mahogany table was beginning to annoy Craig—he had to raise his voice to get the attention of the suits at the far end, and three separate islands of conversations seemed designed to plague him. Stock prices flickering across the wide screen against the wall opposite the view of Wall Street teased at the edge of his vision. Felicity sat to his right, thick as thieves with an investment banker whose name appeared on the Morgenthau Pierce stationary.

"Vanguard has already spoken for a 4 percent share, and Fidelity requested another 2 percent stake for one of their small cap funds. With investment parameters we're going to outgrow by..." She paused to examine a series of graphs with steep curves. "By next month. If all goes well."

"It will," he assured her. "It's a real pity you decided to retain such a high percentage of the stock. We're oversubscribed on the institutional end. I imagine the play on the open market will lift..."

Craig quit paying attention—he'd heard this chat or variations of it too many times already. Yes, he could float another ten percent of the company and funnel even more millions into his pocket, but why? He liked control, and no investment banker with his eyes on the dollar signs was going to create a situation where Craig couldn't cast the deciding vote. Being answerable to shareholders was enough of a chafing restriction—he'd built this company and damned if he'd let someone else tell him how to run it.

Then again, perhaps he should outwait the holding period, sell his entire stake, and plow the billion or so dollars into the kind of project he'd been tossed out of way back when. Bring back something desperately needed and still thrown aside, because the company with the money had a greater need to shut it down. A man needed a challenge.

He'd built SecurNow from scratch with the proceeds from the sale of Quatnatics, hadn't he? A startup was pretty nearly the only way he knew of to part with as much money as he'd walked away with: it was certainly too much for one person to spend on himself. He could stay in the Vivaldi penthouse indefinitely on his current assets, even at the correct door rate, which he'd looked up out of curiosity. Joshua could assist him in spending his wealth and still not run through his resources unless he developed a collector's taste for fine art and racehorses.

Which he might—it could be fun to cheer on his own Derby winner.

Except then he'd have to learn everything there was to know about a new and unrelated field, because he hadn't built his current empire on guesses and ten-year-old data. Nope, no horses for Craig, but something to hang on the living room wall that properly belonged in a museum ought to put a decent sized hole in his wallet. Something by Monet, perhaps, or Picasso, although it might be more fun to set off on a collection of Sauviere. Probably shouldn't hang nineteenth century homoerotic art in the living room, though.

He could call Joshua and have him find the name of the gallery...

"Craig. Craig!" dispelled his pleasant daydream. Felicity's crossness came through loud and clear. "Are you sure you don't want to increase the public share? Gorman Hogenboom wants a chunk."

"If I recall correctly, that was dealt with months ago and the paperwork is already filed with the SEC. It's too late to make changes." Gorman Hogenboom could buy on the open market like anyone else.

"Not if we delay the IPO," she argued.

"I'm not doing this twice," Craig shot back. "We're ready to rock and roll now."

No, he would not make any changes on the current public offering—he had plans for the money, potential hires lined up, and a deposit on a building in the Denver Tech Center. Felicity's desire for another chunk of money would not be allowed to derail his plans.

A huge wave of distaste for every one of the money people rolled through Craig. He was a tool for their enrichment. He could have been any one of a thousand entrepreneurs and they would have chattered and waved reports the same. He needed to be somewhere else, talking to someone else, someone who wanted more than the fees and the options.

Craig excused himself from the fray, disappearing down a corridor lined with art of the sort that told him they were charging fees well beyond the worth of the service. Why did an investment bank need a series of Manet haystacks that looked entirely too authentic? He pulled his phone out and dialed the hotel.

Playing it cool, he managed to ask for what he wanted. Or part of it. A small part. "Joshua, I know it's short notice, but could you get me two tickets to a show tonight? *Hello, Dolly* for preference, since I haven't seen Bette Midler perform in a while. If tonight isn't possible, *Hamilton* would do. Or *The Lion King*, or *Wicked*. Since I haven't seen any of them. Surprise me. And reservations for a pre-show dinner somewhere closer to Times Square. I'm open to suggestions; you know my requirements."

Joshua was all business, unlike his inquiry at the base of the elevator. "We can do that, no problem. Dinner would need to be early, since curtain is at seven, so, five thirty? Allowing for a brisk walk to the theater, like New Yorkers do. Would Le Bernardin suit? It's a seafood restaurant. Fish is *parev*, so that shouldn't be an issue."

"Except for all that shrimp and lobster." Craig shivered in spite of himself. "Afraid that wouldn't work for me at all. It really has to be kosher."

"No problem. I have a *glatt* kosher sushi bar close to the theaters. Or an Uzbecki restaurant, if you like shish kebabs and kasha. Or there's Shoshana's, that's more upscale."

"Something suitable for a date." Craig smiled. "What would you recommend?"

"Shoshana's, definitely," Joshua told him.

"Then Shoshana's it is. Five thirty at the restaurant, and where do I pick up tickets?"

"At the box office will-call window. I'll text you with the information."

"Perfect. Thank you." Craig closed the call just as Felicity stuck her head out of the conference room to summon him back to the discussions.

"Have we decided anything new?" Craig asked the assembled bunch of suits. "Or are we going around and around on issues I've already declined three times? Because I think we're going in circles and maybe we should all kick back until Friday morning."

"There really is more work to do on this IPO, Craig," Felicity dared speak up into the silence.

"Fine." Craig hadn't moved from the doorway. He stared down the mahogany conference table, meeting expressions that varied from amused to horrified. "Then do the work. If I've already shot the idea down the first three times, don't expect me to sign off on it on a fourth exposure. You will not like what happens next.

"Anything that has already been filed with the SEC is set in stone, and you can fight amongst yourselves over which of your favorite clients gets a larger share. Because I do not care. Do not annoy me with trivial shit. As far as I am concerned, you've been wasting my time for the last hour. Possibly longer, and certainly every time someone's requested a change that benefits someone other than SecurNow. That stops. Now.

"Do whatever you consider 'real work' on this project, and present it to me tomorrow morning, beginning promptly at nine a.m."

Craig surveyed the double row of dropped jaws with a grim satisfaction. Sometimes you had to hit them between the eyes to get their attention. He shot a quelling glance up and down the ranks of bankers. Felicity looked like she might object but wisely swallowed the words. What came out of her mouth was exactly what she should say. "I'll take care of things here, Mr. Ridley."

"Very good, Ms. Van de Bogart. I'll see you tomorrow."

Time to have less crap and more New York.

Joshua rang his favorite ticket broker, hoping against hope for good last-minute seats at the Shubert Theater, because that was Craig's first choice. Score!

His pleasure was as a concierge, not as a man pleasing someone he wanted to impress. No, he'd make it possible for Craig to impress some other man.

Bette Midler as Dolly Gallagher Levi would be an amazing show. Not that Joshua had seen the show. Or had a date to see the show. Craig had asked for tickets as if Joshua was no one and nothing to him.

Quit feeling sorry for yourself—of course you're no one and nothing to him. Two nights of Rent-a-friend did not a relationship make. Even if Joshua provided companionship two evenings in a row. He hadn't billed a cent for last night. Because he'd come back with a Scrabble board and his own dinner for the pleasure of spending an evening in Craig's company.

Damn it.

Someone else would sit across the table for two he'd booked at Shoshana's and eat the roast duck or rib steak. With Craig.

Guess he was good for something, even if it was only for making reservations for Craig to use with somebody else. Joshua'd even dashed up to the penthouse to fold a completely new four-towel per creature sculpture, just to make Craig smile. Bet that would fall flat too.

Damn it.

The phone rang again, a nuisance instead of an opportunity. He let Lauren take it.

She handed the handset to him. "Kosher towel guy seems to like you."

Yeah, right. Enough to have Joshua set up a date for someone else to enjoy. Someone else would listen to stories told in that good-enough-to-eat baritone. Craig had been honest, at least. He didn't want sex, because he had someone.

"Hey, Joshua, I have a problem," barely brought the seething to a level where Joshua could listen.

"In what way?" he managed to ask.

"This is a bit unconventional, but you're the man who can manage it."

Great, back to being the ticket monkey/limo summoner.

"See, I had someone from Rent-a-friend come up and hang out with me a couple of times, but like an idiot, I didn't manage to get his private telephone number, and I don't have any other way of contacting him except through the concierge desk."

"I see," Joshua choked out. "What would you like me to do?"

"Could you check with him, please, and inquire if he's free for an early dinner and a Broadway show? I just got the word that I have a pair of tickets to see the Divine Miss M. Think that's possible?"

"More than possible." Joshua's heart thudded within

his chest hard enough to be heard in Jersey. Keep it calm, keep it calm, Lauren did not need to know how much he wanted this evening. "Any time after five should work."

"Terrific. I'll be back by then, long enough to change clothes and then away we go. And thanks." Oh man, the warmth in his voice…

Joshua's heart hammered double-time. A date? This didn't sound like anything except a date. He'd been asked out. He'd really been asked out!

Lauren dispensed "skip the line" vouchers for the Empire State Building to a suntanned matron who thanked her in a Texas twang before she pounced on his good mood. "So, what happened? You looked like someone kicked your puppy and now you're ready to float away. What did he say?"

"He's pleased with the tickets." It might kill Joshua not to tell his work wife about his date. It was a date, right? Not Rent-a-friend gone berserk. Had to be.

Every phone call now was only a way to tick off the hours until Joshua'd see Craig again. Not snapping at every entitled crybaby who couldn't look up a phone number or issue a direct request themselves took enough concentration to make the time pass at half speed instead of reverse. Did Joshua's entire career involve looking after people who couldn't say, "Siri? Find…"

Maybe it was. And maybe it didn't matter. One such request brought him Craig, and another led him to this maybe-date tonight.

Five o'clock was so damn far away.

But leave-o'clock finally came. Joshua left a hole in the air behind the concierge desk. He blew through the kitchens and back to the elevator banks via the back route, hoping to get upstairs to the penthouse before Henry or a housekeeper or anyone else who knew him noticed. Yes, he should be able to go out with anyone he wanted, but guests were tricky.

The Vivaldi Central Park and its sister hotel downtown frowned on staff fraternizing with guests. But Joshua wasn't doing anything wrong. Sure, he'd slept in the suite twice now, but his mama could have come to tuck him in without blushing. After he'd finished the self-soothing for not being next to Craig.

Now Craig asked him out in this weird, convoluted way. Joshua'd been told to wait until he'd been asked. Now he'd been asked—something.

Whatever, he'd take it.

His knock on the polished maple door went unanswered, so he let himself in with the passcard. With a twinge of conscience—that passcard was for business, and he wasn't here on business. He wasn't. No, he wasn't. Off the clock, free as a bird, own time, all that jazz.

Craig found him a few minutes later, admiring the changing leaves in Central Park, isolated patches glowing red and yellow in the slanted late afternoon light. "You're a sore sight for eyes."

Joshua wanted to cross the expanse of carpet to put his arms around Craig and welcome him home. Which was absurd. This wasn't his territory to announce homecoming, it was his job to offer hospitality, which did not include hugs or kisses or dates.

Which was getting to be a pain in the ass. He could whipsaw his own emotions pretty damned effectively.

"Glad to see you too." He shouldn't get close enough

for Craig's cologne to overpower the lemon furniture polish some diligent housekeeper used earlier. Musky and spicy—he'd already determined the scent should be sold by prescription only. It had already caused a couple of erections lasting for hours. "I didn't give Salvator instructions. Did you?"

Craig waved Joshua to follow him, chatting as he headed to the danger zone, erm, master bedroom. "He's waiting at the front door for us. I wanted to change into something more casual."

Danger, danger, danger. Craig was going to take his clothes off. While Joshua watched and did absolutely nothing about it.

"Did you want a polo shirt or something? It's still quite warm out." Craig hung his suit jacket and pulled his tie off. "Mine would fit, though it could be tight."

"Might be a good decoy—everyone expects to see me in a jacket." Oh man, Craig was such a fucking tease, all unconcerned and nude from the waist up. Looking so fine, with defined muscles in his arms and chest, a light sprinkling of hair over the upper swell of his pecs. Tossing a supple pima cotton shirt Joshua's way. He could barely pluck it out of the air—he needed both hands to hide the wood he'd just sprouted. Turning his back only solved part of the problem. Joshua could not make a big deal out of this. Not even when he could hear a zipper coming down behind him, knowing Craig was smoothing in shirt tails and making himself comfortable.

He stripped off his dress shirt. He'd waited to be asked, all right, and now he was undressing only to cover up again.

Joshua lowered his own zipper, his cheeks blazing. At least he had an excuse to rearrange his erection to what he hoped was an inconspicuous lie. His towel sculpture lacked eyes to watch him shift his dick.

He could feel Craig's eyes on his back. He hoped.

Until the scream.

"Agh!" Joshua felt Craig's recoil as a breeze.

"What?" Had he suddenly developed a huge hairy mole on his back? He craned over his shoulder to find the horror.

"It's a lobster!" Craig regarded the terrycloth balefully.

Joshua turned again, regarding his masterpiece, with a bath towel exoskeleton folded into accordion wrinkles. "Yes. I thought the claws came out pretty well, one washcloth apiece."

"It's a horribly accurate lobster." Craig whipped the tail piece back into a fluffy white rectangle, folded it, and went to work on a claw.

Hokaaayyy. "Isn't this taking keeping kosher to an unreasonable degree?" Joshua helped flap the lobster back into its component linens.

"In my case, no." Craig relaxed visibly once the towels lay folded on the bed. "You could say I was frightened by a lobster as a kid."

"Did Moby Snap, the Great Red Crustacean, pursue you onto the beach?" Joshua couldn't resist holding his hands up as claws and pretending to click them.

"Something like that." Craig patted his pockets. "Shall we go?"

The Lobster Incident at least deflated Joshua's problem, but the short trip across the suite to hang his jacket and shirt let Joshua remember he was wearing clothing that had touched Craig's bare skin last.

"Get a grip," he told himself. "Focus." But on what? The sexy man waiting by the front door, patting his pockets and smiling at Joshua? Or the casual shirt that fit him like paint, smooth, soft, paint, that probably showed the peaks of his nipples. Would Craig like the sight? Or acknowledge it in any way?

Don't get your hopes up, buddy .

They strode across the lobby at what might have been a smidge too close for a "friend with friend" distance. The columned, marble space, now only a hushed and gracious lobby instead of Joshua's place of toil, looked different somehow. Was this how Craig saw it, or any other guest? As a place of beauty and welcome?

Certainly without the small cringe of "don't notice me" Joshua wanted to let bow his shoulders. But no. He stopped working here at five o'clock, he'd changed into casual clothing, and he was the guest of a guest. He squared his shoulders, stiffened his back and accompanied Craig out the door to the waiting Rolls Royce, a vintage Silver Wraith older than Craig. Salvator opened the rear door of the mighty sedan, with not even a twitch to show he recognized Joshua.

He might not. Joshua was a voice on the phone to him, with instructions.

Joshua slid across the back seat and settled against the buttery leather for the first time. How often had he summoned this vehicle to do a guest's bidding?

Craig settled in too, the fluted leather bucket cradling him like he'd been born to it. Or maybe that was his attitude.

"The armrest comes down." Craig flipped a barrier between them and leaned an elbow on it.

Seemed like a bigger barricade than a cushion. Hell with it. Josh leaned his elbow too, and let Craig be the one to tell their driver where they were going and when he needed to return.

"We probably could have walked it and taken the same amount of time as it will take to drive," Joshua pointed out as the Rolls inched through traffic. A crane zone slowed them up even more.

"Didn't even occur to me." Craig seemed genuinely surprised. "We have such a car culture in Denver. Downtown is a pain in the ass, but not—" he peered out the window "—anything like this. You can generally go most of a block even in rush hour without stopping. Unless you're near the baseball stadium when a game's letting out. Plan on being there a while if you're careless enough to get caught in it."

"New Yorkers walk a lot. We have to, out of sheer self-defense. I don't know a lot of people who even own cars." Joshua didn't mention not knowing how to drive. "Good public transportation and nowhere to park that doesn't cost as much as your apartment. It's not worth the hassle."

"Still not sure I want to hoof it down to Morgenthau Pierce tomorrow though." Surely Salvator hadn't lurched his quick stop enough to jog Craig's elbow sideways. Almost close enough to touch. Almost. "If I had taken a room at the Vivaldi Downtown, I suppose I would."

"I'm a little surprised you didn't," Joshua admitted. "Since that's the end of Manhattan where you're spending your time." Glad though he was this fascinating man had chosen the better hotel. Nothing against the Vivaldi Downtown, but Joshua had his pride.

"A few too many romantic notions about Central Park, I think. And a complete lack of understanding about how long it can really take to travel four miles around here. If I spent that much time on the road at home, I could be two counties over." A cab blared, the aggressive bleat cutting off the end of his words. "I don't know if I'll ever get used to people driving with their horns."

"I almost don't hear it."

"Selective deafness," Craig teased, and his elbow somehow scooted over another fraction of an inch.

Joshua held his ground. Were they touching? Almost? Or was it some kind of electrical current jumping the gap between their arms? The almost-contact could drive him mad.

"Shoshana's," Salvator announced, stopping the Rolls. He avoided catching a passing Yellow Cab with his door, a snafu Joshua didn't want to contemplate, and came around to let Craig out of the passenger side rear. Joshua followed, in time to hear Craig's instructions for returning after the show.

"Pick us up on 8th Avenue on the north side of 44th, please." Joshua added details Craig wouldn't know to ask for.

Once inside the restaurant, they settled with menus. How delightfully date-like. Joshua peered over his menu, studying Craig more than the choices for their meal. He read everything twice over, debating the merits of steaks in chimichurri, or with cilantro vinaigrette or... "I've never tasted any of these things."

"Time to expand the palate then." Joshua wanted to hear what the waiter had to recommend. "But we need to keep an eye on the time. They won't hold the curtain for us. Maybe a few of the appetizers, and we can share?"

"Is that how you do a pre-show supper?" Craig went back to studying the upper section of the menu, engrossed now in mushroom ravioli and roasted beet salads.

Their waiter turned out to be someone Joshua knew to speak to, from a visit six months ago at the proprietor's request.

Better yet, the waiter remembered him. "Joshua! From the Vivaldi! Good to see you again. I'll let Susan know you're here." He disappeared with their drink orders and a big grin.

The lady herself returned with plates of tidbits fragrant with juniper and rosemary. "Joshua, darling! How good to see you! It's been far too long! What are you hungry for? I've brought you some duck confit on matchstick veggies, a little something we haven't put on the menu yet."

"Oh, yes! Thank you!" Joshua took an appreciative sniff. "This is my friend Craig, and we have tickets for seven o'clock. What would you recommend?" He turned to Craig. "This is Shoshana, who would certainly know what's good tonight."

"Oh honey," she chortled. "Call me Susan like my friends do. Any friend of Joshua's is a friend of mine." She winked and disappeared in an herb-scented cloud of promises to send out the choicest dishes in the kitchen.

"But what if I wanted the..." Craig trailed off, confused by the welcome but ready with a fork. "Do you know everyone in town?"

"Not everyone, but I'm in the hospitality industry, so I try to know people my clients need to know about. Say, like the man in the penthouse who wants kosher and New York lavish." Joshua paused for a bite of the heavenly duck that all but melted into a gamy explosion on his tongue. "Because I deal with people who want lovely dinners and interesting experiences, people in the hospitality industry also try to know me."

He ate another bite of the duck, enjoying the flavor, but not as much as he enjoyed watching Craig eat. Did he approach everything he put in his mouth with suspicion that turned to enjoyment?

Craig finished the last scraps of carrot and rich meat. "So, they bribe you with duck confit or whatever?"

"Think of it as demonstrating the quality of their product." Joshua rephrased to a more accurate assessment. "It's easier to recommend something when you're certain it's good. I made a few errors in my early days." He'd also caught hell from some clients who hadn't appreciated the watery sauces or chain-restaurant sameness they could have had at home. He'd also learned where to send the particularly obnoxious clients for guaranteed bouts of explosive diarrhea. At the cost of some clients who hadn't deserved being his accidental guinea pigs. He kept a small pharmacopeia in the store room for those folks who insisted on dining at such places.

Their waiter returned with a tray of small dishes, each a few mouthfuls of delight, and a bottle of wine. Craig sipped the wine with a pleased sigh, and not a word of prayer.

"Did you not want to make a *brocha*?" Joshua asked, his own glass poised in the air.

"I wouldn't know how." Craig sipped again. "Do you want one? Where do we get them?"

Why did a man who didn't understand a blessing over the wine or the food insist on kosher meals? Craig examined the first forkfuls of each dish with a certain suspicion before nibbling, but fell to with gusto once he'd tasted and paused.

"You're not really Jewish, are you?" Joshua dared to guess aloud.

"Heavens, no." Craig pounced on a brisket eggroll, a pinky-sized mélange of crisp wrapper and tender beef shreds. "I'm a terrible Presbyterian, don't even show up at the church for Easter unless the parents insist, which they have learned not to do. Although I am psychic. I read minds." He pinched the bridge of his nose, spiking his fingers into some kind of cosmic ray/mind wave detector. "You would like to know why I insist on kosher food."

There had to be an explanation for a requirement so adamant. Joshua picked up a black-truffled quail egg. "Does it have something to do with being frightened by a lobster? All that wavy stuff on their underneath is pretty gross."

Craig let go of his nose and collected his fork. "I wish it were just too many legs and weird gills. The damned things do want to kill me. So do shrimp and crab, and I suppose if I were stupid enough to try them, so would the jambalaya and crawfish pie."

"Allergic, huh." Refusing to darken any door that harbored his allergen still sounded extreme.

"Deathly allergic." Craig patted his pocket again. "Carry an EpiPen at all times allergic. Don't dare go to

Fisherman's Wharf allergic. Ought to carry two, probably, but pockets are only so big, so I stash them around the office and the car."

"Sounds bad." Joshua's fingers went loose around his fork, letting it clatter to the plate. Shit, he could have killed Craig that first night, if they hadn't been so busy bristling at each other about how much they weren't going to fuck.

Craig shrugged. "I live with it. I could wish it were only a matter of eating shellfish myself. That's easy to avoid. But contact is enough to create a problem."

"I see. Kosher restaurants make sense." Even the vaguely Christian in New York City like Joshua had some idea of what was forbidden. No shrimp or lobster would ever make its way into Susan's kitchen. "You must miss bacon though."

"Love the stuff," Craig said cheerfully. "But cooking my own bacon cheeseburger is a very small price for the peace of mind that comes with knowing the chef isn't going to throw my food onto a grill where they were searing shrimp a moment ago. Cross contamination is enough to trigger a reaction."

"That little?" Joshua marveled. He could have folded something besides the lobster, but he'd been so proud of himself for the likeness.

"Thank heavens pollen only makes me sneeze. I do my own shopping, eat my own limited cooking, and don't go out to eat much, because some joker at the next table is going to order peel and eat shrimp. Crimps the social life a bit, but who has time for that anyway? I have a company to run. Suppose I could hire a personal chef." Craig buried his face in his wineglass.

Then maybe New York City was the right place for Craig to be, with Shoshana's and Mikeleh's and delis on every fourth corner. Where they could eat together—Joshua could make any necessary bacon cheeseburgers at home... He opened his mouth to suggest that but Craig turned the subject.

"So, tell me about some of the more insane requests you've had." Taking a mouthful of kasha popper, Craig turned the megawatt attention on Joshua.

Under the spotlight, he had to entertain. "I know where to go if you need to dye your dog purple—"

Craig snorted and had to resort to his napkin. "Purple! Oh jeez! Okay!"

"Or pink." Joshua kept a straight face. "I've hired tame ocelots."

"Don't mix them with the pink dogs." Craig's napkin hovered near his face, all alight with his smile.

"Absolutely not. You won't get your deposit back," Joshua agreed faintly. That party could have gone very badly, what with the purse dogs, now that Craig mentioned it. He shook it off—nothing had happened, after all. Should he tell the story of the 55-gallon drum of lube? No, that one might sound entirely too suggestive, and the issue of commercial transactions between them hadn't reared its ugly head in hours. Besides, he couldn't really tell the story without mentioning walking into the room the next morning to discover what an, erm, rousing success it had been.

Better find something else. If he'd been thinking ahead, he might have a "best of" list ready, but he'd arranged so many odd things they'd merged into a giant stew of "just another day at the concierge desk." Except—

"How well do you know the geography on the coast?" Joshua wouldn't claim any expertise with Colorado or any of those other bumpy states in fly-over territory: he couldn't assume Craig had the background to appreciate this.

"General knowledge, not enough to navigate without a map." Craig turned his fork toward the chanterelle ravioli. "New Jersey's on the other side of a river but I don't know which one. Why?"

Joshua considered what details this story needed. "I guess the important part is that Atlantic City is about a hundred and twenty miles away, figure three hours if traffic's good, which it never is. This, ah, interesting foreign gentleman, who apparently prefers stout briefcases to banks with all those messy tracking numbers, comes to the concierge desk."

Joshua hadn't looked away fast enough when the client opened his briefcase. The flash of green wrapped in mustard-colored straps meant hundred-dollar bills in increments of ten grand, and they'd overwhelmed the few stacks of twenties dressed in violet bands. That case had hefted heavy, too, bringing a grunt of effort when the guest swung it up to the desk.

"The client decides he wants to go to Atlantic City for the evening. Which flat isn't possible. Except, I don't like accepting 'impossible.' Always a way around it, you know? Depending on what else you're willing to cope with along the way, and if parting with a chunk of change isn't an obstacle, which I have to tell you, didn't seem to be an issue for this particular guest. 'Open briefcase, find solution inside' seemed to be his motto. I wrack my brain, wondering where's Scotty with the transporter when you need him?"

"Off clinging to the Klingons, apparently," Craig commiserated, his eyes alight.

Good! Joshua held his audience. "What's the next best thing to a transporter? A helicopter. Which I mention to him, thinking this will put him off. He says sure. Again I'm wracking my brains, because it's evening, maybe chopper pilots stick around late but the front office wants to go home, no one's answering the phone. I end up making about half a dozen calls, including out to Las Vegas, because it's earlier there, I can maybe find someone who knows someone, there's not so very many of these guys. I can tap into the network."

"Makes sense." Craig wrapped his fingers around the stem of his wineglass but didn't lift it. Joshua forced his eyes back to Craig's face and his mind to his story.

"Which worked. It almost always works, you know? My Las Vegas contact gives me the cell number of a buddy of his who runs the heliport down by the Battery, where I called first, but he's probably home with his feet up by now. He tells me I'm a pain in the ass for wanting this at the last minute, but hold on, he can maybe roust one of his guys for my cockamamie idea."

Getting someone to pick up the phone had been the hard part. Joshua hadn't doubted willingness to fly once they heard, "I have a client at the Vivaldi...."

But on with the story.

"He comes back, saying it'll cost me four grand for tearing the guy out of his sweetie's arms, do I want him? Since I've seen inside my guest's briefcase, I figure it's worth asking. Guest says sure. So I escort him up to the roof, we have helipads here and at the Vivaldi Downtown, and about fifteen minutes later, *whupwhupwhup* comes his ride. And I sent him to Atlantic City for the evening. Night. I set him up with a pal from one of the casinos, who made sure he had a good time. He dropped quite a lot of what was in that briefcase on booze and craps or poker, whatever he was playing. He comes back happy, my pal goes home happy, I hear later that the pilot goes home happy. And I haven't had to buy my own hotel room in Atlantic City since."

Craig lifted one brow. "Sounds like quite the evening. Playing gin rummy hardly compares."

"I didn't get to go on that trip myself, I just arranged it. I did get to see your face when I went out when you had a fistful of aces and kings. Not so bad." Not bad at all. Especially since Craig wasn't a sore loser and had laughed for taking the evening's highest point count, unwanted though it was. What else could Joshua do to bring that smile to Craig's face? Being late to the show would bring a frown. Joshua looked at his watch.

"I think we need to run. We need to collect our tickets and it's a four-block walk. Short blocks though, not the long ones." Dashing four long blocks was not an exercise for directly after supper.

"The two sizes of blocks in this city is pretty weird, but okay." Craig pulled himself back from whatever future concierge-assisted caper he might be contemplating. "Let me get the tab, and we'll be on our way." He peered about for the waiter.

Susan reappeared with a plate of blue and lavender macarons. "You two enjoy the show."

"But—" Craig had his hand on his wallet.

"Leave a nice tip," Joshua muttered Craig's way. More loudly, he said, "Thank you, Susan. The meal was lovely as always."

She hugged him against her slightly sauced double-breasted white jacket. "The pleasure is mine. Nice to have you in here again. Now off you go."

Craig set some bills on the table, adding his appreciation with a shake of his head. Once outside and headed down the sidewalk, he said, "So that's what you meant when you said hospitality people are glad to know you."

They dodged a squad of Japanese tourists in T-shirts, all armed with cell phones and taking selfies madly against the theatre district background.

"Feeding me and a friend dinner has a good return on investment. Better than a sign on the side of a bus." Joshua pointed across the street, steering Craig toward the Shubert Theater. "I send seventy groups a day out to dinner. Some of them are going to want what she serves or want it but don't know that until I tell them. And I will. Not just because the food's good. It's because they stand out in my mind. There's a thousand good restaurants in Manhattan."

"I see. Did Mikeleh's feed you too?" Craig headed to the will-call window.

"How do you think I knew how good the short ribs are? Yes, there are other kosher restaurants that I could have recommended. But those samples meant I knew you'd get quality. Do you see something wrong with *quid pro quo*?" Joshua stayed with him while Craig requested the tickets Joshua had reserved and paid for on Craig's credit card earlier.

"I'm not sure."

"Think of it as extremely targeted advertising. Aimed straight at the actual decision-maker." Joshua wouldn't apologize for enjoying the "ads."

Craig still looked dubious, but somehow, when Bette Midler was strutting and singing and holding everyone's rapt attention, he managed to end up ankle to ankle with Joshua.

Joshua didn't hear another note after that.

Chapter Eight

While the back seat of the Rolls Royce didn't see any ca-noodling after the show, Joshua was primed for it. How had such a small contact made such a profound effect on him? He'd had less reaction to sweet things dropping their zippers and brandishing condoms.

Traffic that late was light, and Salvator managed to miss the streets closed off for crane movement. The ride was over quickly. And... he shouldn't assume that Craig wanted more of his company. Not after being told to wait until asked. Even though he'd inhaled Joshua's every word in describing the sights they'd passed on the way back.

"Coming upstairs?" Craig inquired. "Evening seems young still."

"I could probably whip you at Scrabble again." Throw out a challenge, see what happens...

"Twelve points does not constitute a whipping."

Hah! Challenge accepted. "I can make it fifty, even if..." Well, 'even if' shouldn't be an issue. Tomorrow and Friday he was scheduled late. He could run home in the morning, change his shirt and suit, find a tie to match his sure to be sunny mood.

The Rolls pulled away, leaving them standing in front of the revolving glass doors of the Vivaldi. Unpleasantly exposed, really. The doorman was new, and that likely meant he wouldn't recognize Joshua, especially out of context in a less-formal shirt.

Inside, though... Of course Henry would lurk at the bell desk, scrolling on his phone on a quiet evening until summoned to whatever service, or petty crime, he would perform next. Tended to be Viagra and 'extra pillows' this time of night. Joshua didn't want to catch the man's eye. Deb had her eyes down and a phone cradled against her ear, jotting notes. They could scoot right through the lobby...

"Oh, do you have to work in the morning?" Craig let the doorman usher them through. "Are you good with wearing the same suit? We've got ties and shirts already." He grinned.

"Yes," Joshua replied in a quarter of the volume. Their footsteps on the marble blurred his consonants. "Fine."

"Or I could get you something in the morning. If off the rack works. Tailoring would take time." The strains of harpsichord and violins didn't swallow nearly enough of Craig's words.

"That won't be necessary, "Joshua gritted. Damn but anyone who overheard this conversation would be drawing some conclusions.

"I could, if you wanted." Craig reached to the elevator button, his penthouse passcard in hand.

"No, you can't have the concierge send over to Bergdorf Goodman's for a suit," Joshua hissed. Hadn't they been over this? With one eye on the bell desk, he prayed for the elevator to appear before any staff noticed who was standing with the penthouse guest. The location board said "42", "36", and "30", so it could be a while. Please let there not be a lot of inter-floor traffic.

Henry, damn him, noticed Joshua standing at the elevator bank that serviced the upper floors. With a guest.

Bastard! Henry made direct eye contact. That turned into kissy lips. The sound effects didn't carry, but they didn't have to. Nasty smooch noises echoed in Joshua's ears more clearly than if he'd heard them.

Damn it! Henry was rolling an empty luggage cart their way, as deliberately as if he'd been paged. Right up to the adjacent elevator. Like he'd really be hauling some guest's suitcases out when the night, in New York terms, was just getting started.

"Why not?" Craig leaned back, one eyebrow up. "I can afford to pay for my pleasures."

"I know you can, but…" How to explain that he didn't want to be beholden? They were equals right now—Craig may have purchased the theater tickets, and he'd meant to pay for dinner. But Joshua had, even though he hadn't intended to, even though he'd paid with professional credit and future favors rather than currency. Something that Craig, with however many millions to his name, couldn't have matched.

Henry pulled up at the adjacent elevator with his empty cart.

Damn it, not now! He was on his own time, with a companion he liked, and it was none of fucking Henry's fucking business, even if it was in the hotel lobby. Joshua tried to set the bellman on fire with his mind.

But Henry stood there pushing buttons, not bursting into flame. "Freelancing, are we?" he muttered. "Naughty, naughty."

Damn it! Craig's eyes widened at the insult. He swiveled around, ready to lob something that could only end in disaster, whatever came out of his mouth. Joshua grabbed his arm before he could speak.

"Don't mind him, he has filthy notions." Fuck, what if Craig took Henry seriously?

Craig stayed tense, ready to snarl.

"I do not and never have done anything like he's suggesting." By sheer force of will and a gentle shake Joshua dragged Craig's eyes back to his own. "Nor will I ever."

Thank God Craig settled. They didn't need an altercation on any of the surveillance cameras that dotted the lobby. Nothing to get investigated, nothing to expose that Joshua'd already fraternized with a guest more than management would like.

Any more than Joshua liked the doubt on Craig's face.

Buy some time. "I'll have the Rolls ready for you in the morning, Craig." The adjacent elevator chimed and opened its door. Joshua propelled Henry's luggage trolley in, nearly throwing Henry in after it. He hit a random button that would take the car to at least the 26th floor, but not to the 53rd. With a look that promised retribution, he kept the bellman in until he got whisked skyward.

"I'm really sorry about that." Joshua wished he had more words for how sorry he was. Anything to take that look off Craig's face. "He's suggested it. I've told him to shove it."

After a few seconds by the clock and an eternity of hollowness in Joshua's chest, Craig's face softened.

"I want to believe you," he said simply. "And I'd like to punch him, except I suspect that would cause you some problems. So his next tip is twenty-five cents."

Oh, to be a fly on the wall for that! Joshua snorted. "That'll hurt him worse than a poke in the snoot."

"Might have to do it twice then." Craig smiled. "But I see what you mean about problems the hotel doesn't want. However, I still think you ought to come upstairs, deal with a yet to be tailored suit for work tomorrow, and we can finish our evening the way we want."

"Not with Henry laying for me. Once he escapes the elevator he's headed to security to review tapes." Joshua had never been more certain of any prediction. "You refreshing my wardrobe piece by piece to get more company is really blurring the lines between business and pleasure."

"I have money. Money solves problems." Craig poked the button for the penthouse elevator, his reflection dancing in the polished bronze doors. "Still think you should come upstairs."

"It solves some problems." Even as it created others. Like the one keeping Joshua from getting in the elevator. "I had a good time tonight. And I'm not in that business, and don't want anyone thinking I am."

"I see. And I don't." Maybe Craig did see, or maybe he didn't, but damned if the evening didn't end with Craig going upstairs alone and Joshua wearing a borrowed shirt back to his third-floor walk-up, full of people who weren't Craig.

Chapter Nine

Even though he didn't need to come to work until one, Joshua double checked with the Rolls' driver to personally make sure Craig had transport. But nothing else from Craig came through, Deb reported.

Not a peep from him all day.

Should Joshua run up to the penthouse and create towel bunnies? He hadn't been asked. Nor had he billed any of his critters beyond the first one, because that was a service requested by the client. The rest were to bring a smile to a certain man's face.

Craig had requested the dog for Friday. And—that was to make him smile too.

No wonder Craig was unclear on what was a service and what was a gesture between friends. Or would-be lovers. Not that they'd gotten one inch past the smallest contact of footsie. Joshua didn't have it clear in his own head.

The hotel might be right about the "no fraternization" policy—this wouldn't end well. Keep it to service, service, and nothing but service.

Fuck, but he was an idiot. Shouldn't have read anything into Craig's actions.

Craig had spelled it out for him—wait to be asked.

He'd already jumped to conclusions and gotten his head handed to him. And he'd already waited long enough to make him crazy. Shouldn't have read anything into any of this. He was a concierge within these walls, not a man who could find a lover or a friend in the rooms above his head.

His sad bad thoughts didn't keep him from buzzing up to the penthouse to create towel bunnies for each bed. What would Craig think if he left them both on the master bed, humping?

He moped so hard he failed to warn a couple who'd asked for a table at a known gut-buster restaurant. They asked for a table, he provided a table. They didn't ask for advice, he wouldn't give it. Stick to the requests, damn it. And wait to be asked.

Hadn't he been asked for something last night?

If he had, he'd said no.

If this situation got any more fucked up, they'd need the 55-gallon barrel of lube.

Amazing how laying down the law eliminated the bullshit. After removing one senior vice president from the conference room for dredging up nixed ideas, Craig heard a few good ideas, one mediocre idea and only two he had to cut off at ground level. Much better than yesterday, especially without the tech-impaired bloviator who apparently thought that sitting on the board of directors at GeoCities back in the day entitled him to any opinions about SecurNow's operations.

Craig had very good reason for retaining 42 percent control of his company.

Somewhere around mid-afternoon they ran out of new details to chew to death. Craig cut the repeats off with "Ms. Van de Bogart, we have a real company to run to make this IPO worth anyone's time. Shall we?" He offered his elbow in saccharine gallantry, meaning only to shut down the investment bankers still quacking about details no longer subject to change.

To his great surprise, Felicity dropped her iPad into her bag and slipped her hand through the crook of his elbow. "Why, of course, Mr. Ridley. We have a great deal to do. Thank you, gentlefolk. We'll see you at the opening bell tomorrow."

In perfect step, they marched out of the conference room, maintaining the charade until they were safely ensconced in the elevator. They had forty-seven floors of descent to hurt their sides laughing.

"Oh, Craig, you are such a naughty boy!" Felicity managed to honk through her nose in a style not approved of at cotillions.

"They make me tired. Pushing the money around until it puffs up instead of creating a product that anyone wants enough to pay for. Remind me why we decided to do a public offering?"

"Money, darling, lovely, lovely money. Buckets and barrels of money, suitable for server farms and brainiacs to work them, and enough fuel cells to power them until after the sun goes out. All without having to borrow." Felicity sang his song, all right. Exactly why Craig kept her around. "And, perhaps, enough for a theater ticket here or a symphony subscription there. Well, no 'perhaps' about that. Bringing a multi-billion company public merits an afternoon at Cartier's or Tiffany's."

"Have fun with that," Craig told her. Whatever floated her boat. "Tomorrow or Saturday. We really ought to look at the plans for the new Tech Center building. I want to be able to expand the network without tearing apart the entire floor."

Summoning the Rolls would take too long, even though Felicity turned up her nose at a Yellow Cab. "Really, Craig, you have no idea who threw up in here last."

Craig winked at the driver, lest he take off without them. "Okay, let's take the subway. I haven't had that adventure in New York yet."

"You're full of terrible ideas," she scolded, but got in the bright yellow miniature Nissan van.

"Joshua would take me on the subway if I wanted to go." Perhaps that wasn't the wisest comment he'd ever made, but true. Maybe he should suggest it. Maybe he should have called earlier. They'd parted in less than ideal conditions yesterday, but surely Craig had mentioned a need for dinner and a desire for some New York experience with the most copacetic guide. Maybe there was a concert in Central Park, even this late in the season. Carnegie Hall was around here someplace; Joshua would know which maestro was playing.

"Who's Joshua, and why would he do something as plebian as take you on the subway?" Felicity pounced.

"Because I want to go." Craig answered part of her question and ignored the rest. A blare of horns and a lurched stop at a light made a great distraction.

For ten seconds.

"Really, who's Joshua?" Felicity fixed her beady eyes upon him.

Instead of answering, Craig peered upward through the window like he'd never seen a skyscraper before. Playing the staring yokel agog at buildings over forty stories served to annoy her.

Though it didn't impair her memory. "Wasn't that the concierge?"

"Mm hmm." He kept his face to the window.

"Why would the concierge take you anywhere personally?" she demanded, her voice cutting right through the radio's chatter in some unidentifiable language.

"Seems to be the way it works, just like you said." He wouldn't dignify her questions with complete answers, especially when he wasn't entirely sure what they were. But there had to be more than the commercial aspect they'd started with. After everything.

Even after, maybe especially after, their parting last night. Which pissed Craig off, though he understood exactly why it happened. Joshua had a brilliant method of getting rid of their eavesdropper, in retrospect. "I request, he supplies."

"That seems a bit extreme for services, particularly when you have the Rolls available." The atmosphere inside the little yellow van grew even closer than it had been with the garlic and cumin fumes wafting off the driver.

"Might be part of the New York experience to do it once." Craig grabbed an "oh shit" handle when the cabbie hit the brakes especially hard, his hand on the horn. "Just like this cab ride."

"A pity you weren't prepared to wait for the Rolls," she said pointedly.

"We have work to do," he reminded her. "A forty-minute wait and making Salvator slog through this traffic in both directions isn't reasonable." He braced for some verbal equivalent of snapping her fingers at his consideration or knowing his driver's name, but she mercifully turned to pointing out the sights.

Once at the hotel, they crossed the lobby laden with briefcases. Craig checked the concierge stand, where Joshua scribbled furiously, a phone trapped between his ear and shoulder. Hard at work, sweet guy. Making some dreams, or whims, come true. Craig caught his eye long enough for a quick smile, returned with a flourish of a pen.

He was on late again tonight. Craig could work Felicity's fingers to the bone while waiting for Joshua to finish his obligations. Because damn it, if Craig had to wait for the company he really wanted, he'd get the most mileage out of the time.

They spread their paperwork and devices all over the dining table Craig preferred seeing laid with a meal for two, but he was saddled with the paperwork companion and hours of work yet. When he would prefer to be exploring an exciting new city with—someone else who still had hours of work.

Back to the salt mines.

"Accepting the Genesee proposal will potentially save an estimated two million dollars over ten years," Felicity pointed out when they'd compared three plans for revamping the newly-leased building in Denver's busy southern office district.

"What are you seeing that I'm not?" Craig examined the plans, which didn't have obvious money leaks marked with arrows. "I thought Art's plan would work best."

"The materials cost is higher, but the labor for buildout is equal, and maintenance is going to be a lot easier. Look, Art has the main cabling running under cubicle space, not walkways. What are we going to do with everyone who gets evicted from their work areas? Lots of lost productivity there, more than offsetting..." She finished her analysis, leaving Craig shaking his head.

"Obviously I missed some implications of his design changes." Craig rubbed his temples.

"Perhaps his being a friend blinded you to a couple of details." Felicity didn't sound accusing. More sympathetic. "It's possible, even probable, that Art didn't realize it either. I might have signed off on the construction billing had I not thought to check with Joan at LoganAct. They expanded on some of Art's work and ran into snags."

"We can do without future snags." Craig wanted to keep his people happy and busy. "I also wanted to do business with someone who'd done business with us."

"And he's a ski buddy." Felicity twirled her pen. "But Genesee's also had us in to do some cyber-security work."

"Good thing you're alert." Craig stretched and stood up, needing to work out the kinks after so much sitting. The view past the Steinway drew him, with the red and gold-flecked emerald of Central Park unrolling into the distance fifty-three floors below.

"I'm always alert," she agreed, coming to join him at the floor to ceiling window that must have been a bitch to glaze in at this altitude. "But you were starting to mix business with pleasure, so I checked. Because I have your back. Excuse me a moment, please."

She left Craig alone with the view. Mixing business with pleasure—wasn't that exactly the problem he and Joshua had? Craig still wasn't sure how much of their time together was billable through the hotel. He'd check the invoice when he left Saturday, but somehow he suspected the concierge desk hadn't added much other than theater tickets and food to his tab since his first evening here. He didn't want to know.

Felicity headed off toward the second bedroom. Joshua's bedroom. How dare she invade his space—oh yeah. She was avoiding the master bath, respecting Craig's privacy. Not knowing she was invading Joshua's. Sort of. Not really. She had to pee somewhere. He couldn't send her back to the lobby. Even if Joshua's toothbrush stood in a glass by the sink.

Felicity returned shortly, her expression neutral, almost carefully so. "I'm going to ask you to remember I have your back, Craig."

He glanced at her with irritation. "The subject came up about five minutes ago. I suspect I know what you're about to say. Which isn't the same as wanting to hear it."

"You need to, just like you needed to know about your pal Art." She smoothed her skirt, as if the fabric dared wrinkle around Felicity Van de Bogart. "Why are you getting involved here?"

He turned, the panorama of New York insignificant compared to the image of Joshua in his mind. "Because he makes my life easier with what he does. I'm happier for being with him. It could be more. A lot more."

"Oh, Craig." She ran her fingers through her hair, a curiously vulnerable act for this woman of stone. "What you're describing is called 'a wife'."

Perhaps she needed a wind-up for acting human. He'd never seen that before and didn't want to now. "Try not to be ridiculous. Not only do I neither want nor need a wife, the only single woman I'm around a lot is you." In no way had Craig ever considered wives being part of his landscape, except as married to other people.

"Your point being…?" With her chin tucked back like that, she bore a striking resemblance to Craig's fourth grade teacher, or maybe it was that same relentless drilling for answers.

"You don't do wife stuff. You do money stuff. That's the way I want it, that's your place in my life, and it works very well." If Felicity had a softer side, it had never been aimed at Craig, and what would he do with it anyway? "We fight every time we talk about something other than SecurNow. I don't think you have it in you to pick up anyone's dry cleaning but your own."

"I send the housekeeper for the dry cleaning, Craig." Her expression suggested she might not know where the dry cleaners was. "But you might be surprised."

Five steps toward the window had better extricate him from this conversation. Which seemed to be going down hard, like all the way to street level from the fifty-third floor. "I don't need that sort of surprise. What I need to do, as you have so thoughtfully pointed out, is to not mix business with pleasure. It has caused a couple of issues already."

She followed him toward the window. "In this case, it could solve several problems you might not know you have. Socially. In the business world. For posterity. Now that our IPO is almost launched."

Since his biggest social problem was trying to organize time with a certain concierge, it took a couple of moments to sink in. Like lava hitting sea water. Craig hissed. "Wait— You thought— What, that we'd go public and then do something, I don't know—dynastic?"

She smiled. "Think about it. You and I together make a powerful couple. Possibly the next generation of Bill and Melinda Gates. Together we control just under 50 percent of SecurNow, with the wealth and the clout that supplies."

How had Craig not considered he'd become het-bait? Or how much his CFO resembled a shark?

"My social credentials are as impeccable as my math, Craig. I'd make you an excellent wife. I'm your introduction to sitting on the boards of directors of Fortune 500 companies. Charities, if you lean that way. I'm your leverage to doing more than run one company in the middle of fly-over land. You'd have this view from your breakfast table every morning, when we're not in the Hamptons." She stepped closer to the window, gazing down at the world at her feet.

Reeling with this topsy-turvy view of his future, Craig had to step backwards and nearly stumbled. He addressed the most comprehensible bit of nonsense to come out of her mouth. "Wh… why would you even think I'd stay in New York? The business is in Denver."

"True, but that doesn't mean we have to be. We can be anywhere we like. I happen to like Cannes almost as much as New York." She smiled, and if that was supposed to be enticing, she missed.

"Have fun there. Without me. I have a billion-dollar business to run, which I thought you were interested in running as well." Could someone please explain, in small words and with diagrams, how his afternoon had morphed into this conversation?

"It was delightful, Craig, and very good for the résumé, but think. We've built SecurNow, we've launched it, or will tomorrow. It's not money now, it's supermoney, and the management is different. You didn't experience that when you sold Quatnatics. You got cash from Google and spent it on a new company almost before the sale was complete. And it wasn't on this scale."

She turned away from the window. Must be killing her to stop admiring her future kingdom, or maybe she thought she was making eye contact with another part of it. Craig held his ground, a stronger way to describe being pinned against a baby grand piano.

"Once the lockout period expires, you sell, you diversify, and then you kick back and enjoy life at the top." She gestured around the suite, as if Steinways and Kandinsky paintings defined a life worth living. "You can have this kind of luxury, anywhere in the world, and I'd be there, guarding your back, making sure you meet the right sort of people."

The "right sort of people to meet" was the sort of people Craig met, not the sort with money and entitlement. Could Felicity even contemplate that without her skills in finance, *she* was not the right sort of people?

He'd deconstruct the issue for her. "I'm not interested in marrying into society. I know nothing of running a charity, and I won't be a figurehead. I'm not turning into a country club and gala kind of guy. If that's what you want, perhaps you should have cast a wider net among the hets at Harvard."

She waved that problem away with a flick of well-manicured nails. "Dear boys, some of them, but with a different worldview. Comes with being born to money rather than making it yourself. The kind of drive you have harnessed to the privilege they have is how a mover and shaker is born. Did you have political ambitions? We could buy you a district, though you might need a spray tan and a few billion more to end up in the Oval Office on the first round."

Dear God, his head might explode. "No. Absolutely not. Not in this lifetime, the next lifetime, or any lifetime. None of that. Especially the wife part. You may have forgotten, but I'm gay."

Not even a blink. Her eyes never lost that reptilian focus on him, her prey. "Why would that stop us?"

"Seems pretty basic to me." He needed to throw a net over this woman!

"You mistake me for someone who wants into your pants, unlike your concierge." She rolled over his sputters. "You can have your sidepieces, as long as you're discreet and we have a couple of children. We can conceive them without too much damage to your tender sensibilities."

His tender… Fucking hell! "We're talking about people here, not accessories!" Craig yelled. "Dear God, woman! Have you already put a silver turkey baster on a registry at Tiffany's?"

"That's an idea." She smiled most unpleasantly.

"No. Hell no." His stomach heaved. "This is bullshit. This project is dead, vetoed, never to be discussed again."

"So you think your little sweetie Joshua is a better bet for the partner of an extremely wealthy man?" Felicity snapped. "Can he help you maintain the position you've achieved? Of course not, though he'll get you Viagra and a whore. Have you worked your entire life to build something up and then waste it over a piece of ass you just met?"

A red haze spread across his vision. He'd grind this shit into nothingness. Joshua was the opposite of a piece of ass—how dare she? How. Dare. She.

"Ms. Van de Bogart," he ground out. "This is your boss speaking. You will keep his name out of your mouth."

"Fine," she spat back, jamming papers into a bag marked with a subtle logo. "Enjoy your little gold-digger while he lasts."

"Manners, Felicity. Use them." Craig held the door open for her, wanting to slam it into her ass for the second time that week. "Perhaps we should discuss your continued association with SecurNow when we return to Denver. Since you have a hankering to get out of flyover country."

"You need me, Craig, rather more than I need you." She yanked at the door almost harder than he wanted to slam it. "Enjoy being wealthy and all alone. Hope it keeps you warm at night."

She pulled the door to with a muffled thud, as much noise as one could get from such a sound-proofed building.

Craig leaned his throbbing head against the door, breathing hard. How exactly had their conversation gone south so hard and so fast?

He was fine with being alone. Really. Even if he did marry Felicity in order to join the high society, big money lifestyle, which, bleah, Felicity wouldn't keep him warm.

Trouble was, Joshua wasn't keeping Craig warm either.

Craig wanted him to.

Time to call.

Chapter Ten

The call, when it came, was for deli this time. Joshua didn't mind in the least sending someone besides Henry. The bellman had the day off, which suited Joshua just fine. There'd be some sort of reckoning when they met again, and Joshua wasn't looking forward to it. He had clout, he had connections, he made the hotel a lot of money, but Henry had the unofficial blessing of someone higher up, who didn't entirely mind bending the law in the name of profit and guest satisfaction.

No explaining Henry otherwise. Joshua was pretty sure he was the more valuable to upper management, but he wouldn't like to find out he was wrong.

He really didn't want to be a cog in Henry's enterprises.

But the call—Craig, sounding worn, requesting something simple. Pastrami on rye, easy food, but done well from Fromm's Deli. "Get something for yourself, if you'd like," Craig had added, his "and join me" hovering unspoken but understood.

Joshua knocked on the penthouse door, bag in hand. Craig opened at his knock, eyes alight. "Come in! Let me clear these papers, we can sit at one end of the table."

Joshua found a plate and a fork for the potato salad in the gleaming sideboard. Paolina, or perhaps Amaya, had washed up this morning and returned the delicately patterned china and heavy flatware to their cubbies. A service Joshua had only shared vicariously, courtesy of Craig.

The dining table sat in a pool of light in the otherwise dim penthouse. The last daylight was already gone. The lights of the city formed a glittering filigree for the dark jewel of Central Park, spattered with light at the band shell and along the walks. The baby grand piano blocked out a triangle of high rises, becoming part of a skyscape where Joshua was a furtive visitor.

Craig belonged here, with a museum-quality oil painting on the wall. Joshua didn't, unless he was providing a service.

He laid out the sandwich, piled high with thinly sliced meat, at the clear end of the dining table.

"Wow, that is a monster of a sandwich." Craig found the miniature jar of brown mustard in the bag. "No wonder you only bought one. Let's split it to open-face. I'm not sure I could open my mouth wide enough to get the whole thing in. You do like brown mustard?" He divided the stacks of pastrami and started slathering.

Joshua found a napkin in the bag and added it. One napkin.

Craig noticed. "Why one?"

He had to say the words. Joshua swallowed hard. "I have to get back downstairs."

"Because you're working late tonight?"

"Even if I wasn't, Craig."

"But..." Craig set the mustard down. "This is connected with last night, isn't it?"

Joshua nodded, not wanting to meet Craig's disappointed eyes. "It is. I may have a major problem with Henry. I can't risk making it worse. I'm damned if I do and I'm damned if I don't, and what I want doesn't figure into it. Because what I want is to sit down over a meal with you, and ask you how your day went, what would you like to do tomorrow. Tell you stories. Stuff like that."

"Is he really trying to recruit you?" Craig stared, the knife dangling from his fingers. "Has he paid any attention at all to what kind of person you are?"

"No. Do you think it matters to him?" All that mattered was what sort of hook Henry could get into Joshua.

"Fuck Henry," Craig spat. "Or don't, I mean, oh hell, I'm tangling this up. But no." He smacked the knife down on the edge of the plate with a dangerous *chink*. "It stinks that he's bothering you. It shouldn't matter that you're taking a dinner break with me."

"I wish it didn't, Craig. I'd like to hang with you for a half an hour and come back upstairs once I'm off and watch a movie or something. But it does matter." Joshua started folding the deli bag, adding more folds and creases until it became a block of white paper. Something, anything, that he could affect exactly the way he wanted it.

Because he was going to have to say the words. Explain. It might not break Craig's heart. But Joshua would do one hell of a number on his own.

"We have this weird friends slash host and guest relationship. It's all muddled, and in a more perfect world, we'd get it sorted out. It would be easier if you weren't staying in the hotel, except how we're together at all is from you being here." Damn it. Every single minute of the time they'd spent together came from Craig requesting a service.

Didn't matter that Joshua had reversed the charges on Craig's card for that first night, so he could tell himself that the rent-a-friend issue was gone. Except it would always be there, while Craig was a guest in Joshua's hotel. Which he wouldn't always be. "You're leaving. You're going back to Denver. On Saturday."

How had the prospect of a tasty meal with a man who was quickly becoming Craig's favorite companion ever turned into a bleak reminder of his time limits?

"So, even if we're friends, you don't think we could take it any further?" How much further had Craig envisioned taking things with Joshua? He'd snapped at the rent-a-friend on that first evening and spent every night since thinking about how Joshua was becoming so much more.

"You did say I should wait to be asked." Joshua had tormented the bag as small as it would fold—now it blossomed outward when he let it go. "I won't lie and say that I didn't—don't—want to be asked, but this whole thing is such a mess. Even without that shithead Henry. We barely know each other. You're leaving. And I'm not a one-night-stand sort of guy."

"Neither am I." Craig wanted to break something out of sheer frustration. "I don't meet so many people I actually want to spend time with. I meet even fewer I like well enough to start thinking of getting intimate with. Then I meet you."

He swallowed hard. "I have no right to ask you to upend your whole life to come with me. But I can replace your income, let you do whatever you like, as long as you'd like to do it in Denver."

The sideways beady-eye Joshua aimed at him meant he'd fucked up. Basically suggested Joshua would be a kept man. Well, Craig would keep him. Long enough for them to decide if forever would work. But not at the cost of Joshua's pride. "Or—there's a Vivaldi in Denver. The Brown Palace. Or the Hotel Teatro. Five star hotels where I wouldn't be a guest."

Joshua ripped a strip of his fidget bag. "Where I wouldn't be a concierge, either. It's a different city. No contacts, no knowledge. I'd have nothing that makes me able to do my job."

"There really has to be some way to make us work." Damn it! He had enough money to solve any problem— that could be solved by money. Every problem he had with Joshua was compounded by money. Craig would have a better chance if he was a maître-d at a steakhouse than he did as the CEO and major stockholder of a Wall Street darling.

Turning away to trash the shreds of the deli bag, Joshua let his shoulders slump. Craig said nothing—he didn't have the solution to this problem, he had to wait for the concierge in Joshua to find the way to fulfill their desires. When he faced Craig again, he was slumped as before.

"I've known you four days. I don't know how to make an 'us' happen without blowing up everything else in my life." He gestured around the penthouse. "This isn't your life. You have a business to run and it's out west. You're not transplantable."

"Not according to some." Why couldn't Felicity have seen what Joshua saw so readily? "But no, not short of relinquishing what I've built."

"I don't even know how to get us to a place where we know nuking my life is the right choice." Joshua screwed the cap back on the miniature mustard jar. "Skype and a lot of travelling maybe, but it's not the same. If every time we're together is a vacation, how do we really know?"

"What else is there? I just developed a huge need for a private jet. A Challenger 600 with two pilots, fuel, maintenance, shouldn't run more than a couple million a year." Craig tried to take Joshua's hand. "You get weekends off, don't you? I'm the boss, I can set my schedule."

Joshua took a step back. "I don't usually have weekends. Sometimes Saturday, sometimes Sunday. And a day during the week, that may or may not disappear. Craig, you can't be serious. That's way too big an investment for someone you've known less than a week."

"If I don't have a problem with it, why would you have a problem with it?" Craig did some quick math in his head. "Let's say we manage to see each other every other week, we can take turns travelling. That's, hmm, around 200 flying hours, which would run me about the same if I chartered. Not so bad, really. Worth every penny to not go through security at the airport, it's a faster plane, no waiting for baggage. I mean, first class isn't bad once you get on the plane, but the other crap doesn't go away, and that's what makes travelling so exhausting. Totally different experience, and half the time. We could do it."

"You could do it. Not so sure about me—I charter planes for other people." Joshua glanced at his watch. "Craig, I have to get back downstairs. I took this delivery away from a bellman, and he was pissy about it. But I can't stay up here forever, too many people are jumping to conclusions as it is. But I had to talk to you."

Damn it—the Henry problem hadn't resolved. Money would fix that, if Craig's principles ran to paying goons hush money. It would never end, and they'd always want more, and they'd expand their reach if they could. Kind of like government agencies. There had to be a different way to keep Henry's hooks out of Joshua. "Here's a concierge thing—can we hire someone to break Henry's fingers? If there isn't another way to convince him to keep away from you?"

That got a bark of wry laughter. "Rental thugs are Henry's department."

"Well, hell." Craig might have to buy a substantial chunk of Vivaldi Inc. and become the sort of meddling shareholder that could embarrass management into dumping an employee. Which would take time. The lockout period ran nine months, and then he'd have to sell off carefully, notifying the SEC at every step… What had gone so wrong that his buddy Bill bought a stake in a hotel chain? Or was that simple diversification? "Could you switch to a different hotel?"

"There's Henrys everywhere. And they talk to each other." Joshua visibly gathered himself. "Craig, I'm sorry. I have to go. I wanted to tell you I've enjoyed your company. A lot. More than anything. I wish we could make this work, somehow. But I don't see how. So—I'm sorry."

He might as well have punched Craig in the gut. The first man in years he wanted, and Joshua was saying good-bye before they'd started? "We're not even going to try?"

"I don't know how we can, short of one of us getting a life transplant. Or a personality transplant. Or something major, like a pride-ectomy." Joshua glanced around the penthouse, his eyes flicking from picture window to picture window. "I make good money, but not CEO money. I don't even own a studio apartment to bring you back to for privacy. I can't hold up my end of a life on this scale."

"You don't have to!" Craig ground out. "You want a penthouse on Park Avenue? Let's go shopping. You'd know the best realtors, right? It'll shorten your commute."

Joshua smiled sadly. "Like I said, a pride-ectomy." He held up one hand. "Trust me, Craig. It's better to end this now. Before we get into each other so deep that we get hurt."

Damn it! The one man Craig wanted, and he was calling quits. "Too late, Joshua. At least for me. And you haven't even kissed me yet." He dared take a few steps nearer, as if he could defeat Joshua's pessimism with proximity. "Would you at least kiss me before you go?"

With one hand over his lips, Joshua defended his honor. Or something. "I can't."

"Why?" Would this provoking, fascinating man frustrate him at every turn? "Or—you won't. Which is your right. Sorry. But damn it."

"I shouldn't. On every level. Because I had shrimp for lunch." Joshua kept his hand over his mouth. "I probably shouldn't even breathe around you."

What the fuck? "You know what the problem is." Craig took a couple steps back, away from the man who could throw him into a medical emergency. "But thanks for not giving me anaphylaxis. Because that would be the perfect ending for this shit storm of a day."

"I know." Joshua dropped his eyes. "That's why."

How twisted could this get? Joshua, whom he trusted, had gone to the shellfish side. "I don't understand."

Joshua met Craig's eyes. And broke Craig's heart. "Because if I hadn't, I'd wrap my arms around you and stay."

Chapter Eleven

The Jumbotron-sized ticker board flashed blue numbers over the trading floor at Morgenthau Pierce. Streams of digits chased themselves across the screens towering above the raucous men and women shouting into phones and clattering on keyboards. Even though the trading day was less than half an hour old, the room had already taken on a fug of competing colognes and a whiff of fresh sweat.

The blare escalated the throbbing in Craig's temples. His pulse thudded against the back of his eyes, every heartbeat threating to push them from their sockets to roll across the floor. Why did he have to be here? Nothing he could do now would change the course of money flowing.

They'd planned. They'd worked their asses off. They'd built SecurNow into a powerhouse of cybersecurity, and now the money people were turning all that work into wealth. "SCN" raced after numbers on the big board. The first time—19. The second, 19.5, and after that so many more they blurred in his vision, all 20-somethings.

Another trader shed his jacket, still yelling into his headset. So many bodies pounding with adrenaline generated heat. Sweat beaded against Craig's hairline.

He popped his top shirt button and pulled his tie away from his throat. Even that small movement brought back his private pain. He'd chosen the magenta silk that last graced Joshua's throat.

Joshua should be standing here with him. Holding his hand. Sharing in the triumph. But he wasn't. Joshua wasn't even a voice on the phone.

Instead he had a wandering babble of vice-presidents and project managers barging through the madhouse to shake his hand and yell encouragements at the climbing stock price.

Craig tugged at his collar again—even the state of the art ventilation at this old-money investment bank's spanking new headquarters wasn't up to convincing him there was enough oxygen to go around. The drums beat inside his skull. Rubbing his palms against his eyes didn't help. "I'll keep track from the conference room."

His triumph. His big day, a milestone for the company he'd nurtured from a two-desk idea to 600 employees, all newly wealthy. All turned out in this circus of traders—he had enough stories to take back to the men and women doing the work that made the company possible. He didn't need to be here watching the chaos.

"Here, Craig." Felicity chased after him, catching up once he'd shut the pandemonium on the other side of the elevator door. Or perhaps she'd been dogging him all the way across the trading floor and he hadn't been able to hear her. "I have ibuprofen for you."

He dry-swallowed the bitter tablets she produced from the Tardis that was her handbag. "Thanks. I don't know how they think in that racket."

"Perhaps they don't, and it's all reflexes and adrenaline." She followed him into the conference room they'd inhabited all week, empty of people now. The gleaming mahogany table was neatly set with legal pads and pens, downturned water glasses and mints standing witness to the process that would start all over again next week, chewing on someone else's dream.

That was the cycle, wasn't it? Someone created, the bank monetized. They'd all get together to eat filet mignon and drink champagne to celebrate, and then the bankers would turn to the next fountain of money.

She flicked on the wide-screen television, which silently spat ticker symbols and prices. SCN appeared, showing big blocks selling for high prices. "Looks like we're quite the hot ticket. We opened two points higher than the initial quote, and up two points since. A lovely start. Much better trajectory than Snapchat's IPO."

"Perhaps because we do something a little less evanescent?" Every protection SecurNow put in place had to stay—old threats didn't fade away, they were joined by new ones. "I'm just glad it's done. We'll get started on the expansion once we get back to Denver." He cleared his throat, debating whether to offer an olive branch. She was a fine CFO. If she'd just be content to remain CFO… "That is, if you're coming back to Denver."

"I am." Felicity smiled with one side of her mouth. "We have so much to do with SecurNow."

"We do." Felicity could help him accomplish so much, if she'd stay in her own lane. "Or I could sell it all and go live on a desert island."

She smiled. "You'd quickly go mad with nothing to do."

Good point. He'd never stay still. "I could start something new up. Maybe plan for a resurrection of something old. Or learn to scuba dive."

"Even with all those crabs running loose?" She patted her messenger bag. Did she still have an EpiPen in there?

"Okay, I could go live in the mountains. In Aspen, or Wapiti Creek. Improve my skiing." Something, anything, that wasn't New York City with Felicity. With Joshua, now that was a thought....

"Alone?" She lifted one eyebrow.

Yes, damn it, alone. Unless he could persuade Joshua... Yeah, right, like he had a new life for Joshua in his hip pocket, one that his maddening not-boyfriend wanted.

Craig said nothing but gazed out the window at the cityscape below them. Because he would never do more than crunch numbers with her.

"Trouble in paradise? Already?"

Craig turned to snap, but Felicity was quick with backpedaling. "Sorry. That was in bad taste. Unworthy of me. I shouldn't have said anything." She took a step closer to him—why hadn't he put the width of the conference table between them?

"Craig, I'm so sorry I shouted at you last night. I really do know better."

Know better than what, that the way to his heart didn't lie through society? And required a penis? Attached to a man named Joshua Hannes? Who had turned around last night and left. "Don't bring it up again, and we'll be fine."

The lift of her chin and intake of breath might presage an argument, but she uncorked nothing, just patted his arm in a most unromantic way. "We'll be very fine, Craig. Give it a bit."

How dare she patronize him? "Give what a bit?" He jerked his arm away. "Do you think I just need time to process your plan and then I'd agree with you on the joys of life on the Social Register? That isn't who I am."

"You could be."

She withdrew her hand slowly, as if it were her idea and not his that she stop touching him. Pinching the clasp of her messenger bag, she spoke softly, precisely, meeting his eyes with utterly level gaze. "You know I have your back. You'll see I have a point. You're at a new level of wealth now. The rules are different, and you don't know them. You need a guide, and I can do that for you, because I'm a native in this jungle." Barely blinking, she reasserted everything he'd told her not to mention.

"You assume I'm going on your safari. I'm not." Not with her. She was the representative of everything that was wrong with the city outside the forty-seventh floor window. Too many people in too small a space, with too many layers and too many rules, all of them wrong for him. "You were given one directive. One."

"One foolish directive, Craig." She regarded him steadily, waving a well-manicured hand to the spectacular but foreign view from the top of the building. "You're on your way to being so much more than *nouveau riche* in a cow town."

This was too much—she didn't have to diss his life. Craig snarled, "I'm going back to my cow town and live my cow town life with my cow town company that keeps your precious Big Apple and the rest of the world from getting hacked. I'll manage on my own, thank you very much."

He wanted nothing so much as to be outdoors, where the air didn't smell like Felicity's perfume and the warning sounds meant a murderous taxi rather than the death of his future. Even if he had to ride 500 feet down in a cage he had to wait for. Hell with it—Craig knew where the stairs were The door swung shut on her genteel semi-shout of his name. He could do without the sound of her voice forever.

Endless concrete steps echoing downward finally took him out a heavy fire door into the marble lobby opposite the fountain surrounded by bamboo. Salvator wouldn't be here with the Rolls for the better part of an hour even if Craig summoned him right now, and the stairs hadn't done more than take the edge off his wrath.

Because he was going back to Denver tomorrow.

Alone.

Joshua'd made that so clear.

But there was tonight.

Craig pushed his way through the near-silent revolving door and out onto the sidewalk. Enough warmth radiated from the concrete to be felt through the early autumn air, flavored with gasoline fumes and a faint underlayment of rot. Something rumbled through a grate under his feet.

He couldn't stay here, not in this city that wanted to change him. Four miles back to the hotel—to Joshua. Who didn't want to change him, but who Craig couldn't ask to change.

Might be an interesting four miles. With nothing worthwhile at the end, not even a dog folded out of towels.

Joshua'd promised one for Friday, but Craig didn't expect him to follow through. Not after last night.

One foot after another. Craig set off north-northeast, and hoped he'd miss any bad neighborhoods. Maybe he'd see the Empire State Building along the way.

He checked his phone for a map, and then called the concierge desk at the Vivaldi. Joshua answered.

"Hi, Joshua. It's Craig. Um, could you please tell Salvator to cancel the three o'clock pickup? I'm coming back early on foot. I'll need to get from the hotel to the Vivaldi Downtown around eight tonight, though. The big party for the IPO launch, you know."

"No problem." His voice was cool and professional. "What about returning?"

"Not sure." Craig might stay an hour, or all night. Depending on what Joshua said next. "Morgenthau Pierce is throwing a big bash this evening. To celebrate the IPO. Would..." He had to clear his throat. "Would you please come with me?"

He stumbled over a crack in the sidewalk and nearly pitched into a couple of women in business suits and sneakers while waiting for a reply.

"I wish I could. But——"

"Yes, it's last minute and you'd need a tux, it's black-tie, but you could call Barney's, have them send over something in your size——" Craig tried to out-think Joshua's objections.

"I'm working, Craig. I'm on until eleven. And even if I wasn't..."

The one objection Craig couldn't buy his way out of. "I really wish you could be there." To share the glory that would shine bright with dollar signs and accomplishment. He knew which one Joshua would value without asking.

"I wish I could too. But you know why I can't."

"I know."

The hell of it was—he did. Why did the very thing Craig could love most about Joshua be what kept them apart?

Joshua set the phone down slowly. Lauren glanced up from her call, her eyes both worried and full of questions. Nothing he wanted to talk about. Not when he had a lump in his throat too big to speak around. Not when he'd have to say he'd turned down an evening on the arm of the man he was falling for. The man who was so far out of reach it wasn't funny. The man who could be his—until midnight. Or morning, if he wanted to break his own heart. And not one minute after Craig's plane flew away.

If Joshua stayed at the concierge desk, he'd explode.

Swallowing down the blockage, Joshua found an out. "I have a request to fulfill. Back in a couple."

He did have an obligation. So what if he was only torturing himself? Across the lobby and up to the fifty-third floor, where terry towels waited to be sculpted into the man's best friend Joshua wished he could be.

A puppy grew under his hands, wrought with twists and tugs. A puppy to bring Craig the only pleasure Joshua could offer now. A promise kept.

Only one, because to fold a second for the other bedroom was to promise too much. That Joshua would come back. He couldn't.

He stood in Craig's bedroom now, a room he could only enter for business. Beside the king bed that had held the man who could make Joshua break his own rules. The bed he'd never share with Craig. The bed that wouldn't see Craig sliding between the sheets tomorrow night.

Something tickled at Joshua's memory when he dialed the chauffeur, enough to make him end the call before anyone answered. Instead, he dialed the sister hotel's concierge desk. "Hey, Max, I have a guest in the Rolls headed to a party there tonight. Which door should Salvator drop him at?"

"Use the Church Street door," Max advised him. "Have him come through Vesey Street. There's construction on Barclay and the street's blocked off after seven."

"Thanks, Max." Joshua had everything he needed, but his colleague wasn't ready to end the chat.

"So, your man's coming to the Morgenthau Pierce affair?"

"He's the reason for the party." Joshua could be going too…

"Swanky party, even by Vivaldi standards. They're setting up now in the Malachite Ballroom. The leftover roses'll provide enough romance for three hotels. Need any?" Max snickered.

"No thanks, all good here." At least for rose petals. "Thanks. I better let my driver know about the construction." Joshua ended the call before Max could offer any more snark.

Joshua relayed the information to the chauffeur, who gave fervent *gracias* for knowing where the snarls would be.

Maybe, in some other version of his life, Joshua would be on the arm of the guest of honor, instead of the concierge arranging the limo.

Chapter Twelve

Four miles on foot, dozens of congratulatory phone calls, and a trip to the top of the Empire State Building, because a guy ought to see the sights before leaving town, right? Craig would have enjoyed the impromptu sightseeing a lot more with a companion named Joshua, but... Not everyone had the luxury of taking Friday afternoon for fun.

He must have overlooked a dozen interesting things along the way, places only a native New Yorker would know about. Fifth Avenue still offered plenty to gawk at. Craig side-eyed the Tiffany storefront two blocks from the hotel, images of silver turkey basters dancing in his head. Would Joshua even think of shopping there, or would he direct Craig to some smaller, select retailer that required a password to enter? He managed to burn enough time getting back to the hotel that he'd have to jump directly into the shower.

Craig paused, waiting for the elevator, watching Joshua give some other guest tickets and undivided attention. Too far away to hear what he said. Joshua's words would be the same kind of utter professionalism he'd retreated to with Craig.

"If you want him, I'll send him upstairs."

Craig jumped at the words from behind. "You'll do no such thing, you pimp." He whirled to face the bellman, who'd better not wheel his cart into the elevator to the fifty-third floor. "He's none of yours."

"Today." Henry smirked. "We'll see about tomorrow. Since he seems to have popped his cherry with you."

An elevator for floors 2-25 chimed and spread its doors. Henry disappeared into it before Craig could lay him out flat with words or fists.

Damn it! He'd bought Joshua a peck of trouble and all for nothing. There must be something he could do. Craig let himself into the penthouse, empty of the man he'd like to find on the supple leather couch or trying to pick out a tune on the Steinway.

A towel animal waited on the master bed. The puppy Joshua promised.

Craig picked it up, squishing to keep anything from unrolling. Joshua'd said, "A puppy on Friday," and hadn't let last night stop him from keeping his word.

Such a man wouldn't be content as a sidepiece to a lover who'd married for show. Joshua would both want everything and give his all.

Craig clutched the puppy to his chest. There must be something he could do to keep Joshua in his life. Out of Henry's grasp.

Which was the most important thing right now—his eye fell on the sleek black phone on the bedside table. He dialed a single zero. "I need to speak to the general manager," he informed the young man who answered. "No, you cannot help me. I insist on speaking to the general manager."

Perhaps he would get quicker results if he was down at the desk in person, intimidating this Tyler on one hand and slipping him a fifty with the other. "Am I not making myself clear?"

Should Tyler ever relocate to the Mile High City, Craig would hire him as an administrative assistant based solely on his dedication to keeping callers from reaching his boss. However, Craig could out-stubborn the best of them and had the moral high ground of being an unhappy guest, as he reminded Tyler twice.

"You seem to have a prostitution problem in this hotel," he informed the GM, who tutted and made shocked noises. "I had in no way intimated that I wished such services, but your bellman Henry still offered to send a young man up to my room. This is a high-class operation, or it's supposed to be, and he's trying to pimp out his coworkers. What kind of place are you running here?"

Craig chewed on this shithead Grant Wetzel a while longer, hampered by not calling Joshua by name. He'd been jumpy about official notice for completely innocent activities. Craig couldn't throw him under the bus. "I've used the concierge desk for meals and theater tickets, and they all seem quite professional. Exactly opposite of your bellman."

Even after hammering on Henry's inappropriate offer, Craig wasn't sure Wetzel understood the problem. Not when he seemed to be asking if Craig preferred a woman—he weaseled around Craig's fury in being approached at all.

"This Henry is a disgrace to your hotel," Craig snapped. "He should not be offering anything illegal while wearing your uniform. Disgusting!"

With the unpleasant feeling that he'd have to liquidate some SecurNow stock in order to buy enough Vivaldi Inc. to make a complaint stick, Craig listened to the jerk mouth what sounded like useless platitudes. Or—he thumbed his phone quickly and found more ammunition. "You do know who your majority shareholders are? So do I. One of them is a good friend. No, not the Sheik, the other one. I'm sure he and Melinda will be fascinated to know what's going on here. You'd best have your ducks in a row when that call comes in from Seattle."

He couldn't tell platitudes from gibbering at this stage, and he'd said all he could to stir the pot. Would it be enough? Would it be soon enough? Wetzel hadn't actually made sense for six or seven sentences. The man Craig intended to inform wouldn't tolerate word salad for answers. He'd want to know, even if the property involved was a minute percentage of his holdings.

Craig cut the GM off mid-blither with, "Clean up your hotel," and smashed down the receiver. Only the towel puppy in his arms remained to comfort him. He clutched the critter against his chest, the fresh cottony scent wafting into his nostrils when he really wanted the vetiver and musk of Joshua's cologne, underlain with the warmth of his skin.

Craig hadn't stirred from the side of the bed with his terry comforter when his cell rang. A number he didn't recognize, but that was hardly the first time today. He should have turned the damned thing off. Some need for a human connection made him answer, though if it was a telemarketer offering cut-rate cruises he might fling the slender device at the wall.

Congratulations, not a sales pitch, and from the man he'd just referred to! "Yes, thank you. I'm sure we're going to grow. Hey, tell your guys not to leave so many security holes for mine to guard, okay?" They both laughed, and before the call could end, Craig redirected his caller. "I'm staying at your hotel, by the way. The one in Midtown. The suite is lovely, the concierge has been a huge help. Love the Rolls, might need to get one. One problem, though..." By the time Craig finished explaining, the storm clouds in Seattle had doubled.

His call ended with a promise Craig could rely on. Hell would rain down on Henry and the GM come Monday. Joshua would be safe.

But not in Craig's arms.

With a weary sigh, Craig settled the terry pup on the bedspread. More towels hung in the bathroom—he could shower without unfolding Joshua's last gift.

Half an hour later Craig was freshly shaven, clad in crisp cotton and well-draped wool. Rory Patterson had made this tux himself—Craig would have loved to take Joshua to the tailor for bespoke clothing—he'd appreciate the handwork. But that was a dream for another universe.

Craig's bowtie was symmetrical, his grandfather's cufflinks properly latched. Even the onyx studs in his shirt had cooperated, and a good thing, because Joshua wasn't here to help him dress if they wouldn't button properly. One last accessory—he tucked the EpiPen into his breast pocket. Couldn't be too cautious, even though he'd specified that the celebration menu contain no shellfish.

With a final shot of his cuffs, Craig turned away from the mirror. Onward, to the party, and here's hoping he could keep Felicity from clinging to his arm in a more than CFO-ly way for accepting their accolades.

Who else did he have to share his triumphs with? No one. No one who'd meet his news with a kiss. No one who'd hug him until he couldn't breathe and then thump his back just for goodwill—and not ask for a share of the loot.

Or ask him to change everything about himself because of it.

His trip through the lobby lasted years—he shouldn't turn to see if Joshua's eyes were upon him. But he did, one quick glance, and lifted one corner of his mouth. *I wish you were coming with me. But I understand why you can't. And I hate it.*

And maybe, just maybe, Joshua's brief smile meant the same.

Chapter Thirteen

Watching Craig stride across the marble checkerboard floor alone was a knife to Joshua's heart. Head held high—was it confidence or not wanting to glance a second time across the lobby to the man who'd told him no? The knots in Joshua's guts tightened another notch—he wanted to yell, "Wait!" and pelt across the slick marble to slip his fingers through Craig's.

In a more perfect world, he'd be matching Craig step for step, in formal leather shoes and black tie. He'd be getting into the limo beside Craig and heading off to a gala meant to celebrate him.

Not watching Craig disappear through the revolving door and into the waiting Corniche, while phones rang and guests demanded last-minute tables at fully-booked restaurants.

Joshua tore his eyes away from the elegantly-clad figure of the man he couldn't have, casting his gaze down on his list of phone numbers and maître-d's names. The print blurred together into a fuzz of black. He let Lauren field the next call while he struggled with the lump in his throat.

She performed a small miracle, hung up, and turned to him. "What's wrong? Did rent-a-friend go south?"

"More like crashed and burned." After soaring up into the stratosphere and turning six loop-de-loops. Joshua had carried a linen handkerchief for years without ever wiping his eyes on it, but first time for everything. "Not a service we'll be offering again."

"Hey." Lauren slipped her hand around his elbow. "I'm sorry." She leaned her head against his upper arm. "He seemed like a nice guy. You were happy."

He crushed her hand against his side. "He is. And I was. And he's leaving tomorrow and that's that. So…" He shook her off before her sympathy undid him completely. "How many Taylor Swift tickets do you think we're going to need? I have ten requests so far. Think we should buy a block?"

She let go and slid back into pro mode. "I need eight, and the concert's a month away. So yeah, and we should book a party bus, because heaven forbid they walk the twenty blocks to Madison Square Garden."

They lapsed back into work chat, punctuated by phone calls and guests collecting tickets and vouchers. Joshua ignored Henry lurking near the concierge desk. He had nothing to say to the bellman, or nothing that could be said without fists. Of course the little shit had to sidle closer during a lull in the sea of guests.

He waggled a slender yellow cylinder about five inches long between thumb and forefinger. "Heya, Lauren. Isn't this worth about three hundred bucks?"

"Is that an EpiPen?" she asked. "Um, yeah."

No—it was worth a man's life. "Where'd you get that?" Joshua snapped around to glare.

"Someone dropped it on the sidewalk. Right near the Rolls." Henry waggled the EpiPen again, just out of easy reach. "What's it worth to you?"

To hell with the security cameras—he lunged. Joshua snatched a handful of Henry's collar and tie, dragging him half across the concierge desk. He wrestled the EpiPen away from Henry one-handed, more easily for the bellman gasping and clawing to breathe. "It's worth not getting your face bashed in to hand it over."

He shoved Henry away and read the label. Oh fuck: Patient: Craig Ridley.

Craig was long gone.

He had Craig's number in his phone still. Thumbing out a quick warning of "You dropped your EpiPen" didn't seem like enough warning. Not when staring at the screen yielded nothing in the way of response. Thirty seconds seemed like a year.

He'd have to send someone to find Craig, to return the medication. Henry smirked, a harbinger of the crow Joshua would have to eat to get him to go. Two other bellmen lurked at their kiosk—no, one wheeled a laden cart across the lobby, the other had gone God alone knew where.

Technology would be much faster.

A three-digit code brought him "Vivaldi Downtown concierge desk, Max speaking."

"This is Joshua at Midtown. Max, you have to intercept a guest for the Morgenthau Pierce affair. Keep him in the lobby until my bellman gets there."

"I can try. Who am I looking for?" Oh good, Max wasn't asking stupid questions.

"Craig Ridley. He's about five ten, dark hair, mid-thirties, handsome, wearing a tux." Saying "ridiculously good looking, with a voice like chocolate" wouldn't help. Joshua struggled to describe Craig in details a stranger would recognize.

Henry at least would recognize the rightful owner of the pen, but the smugness oozing from his very pores didn't promise a speedy trip.

"That doesn't narrow it down much, Joshua." Was Max chewing into the phone? "Everyone's wearing a tux tonight."

"Clean-shaven, freshly cut hair, very straight nose, looks kind of like Matt Bomer…" Joshua started to panic. What if Craig had already gone by? No—he couldn't have. Not even Salvator could get downtown that fast.

"Joshua, you're assuming I'd recognize Matt Bomer. This is more of a Jim Cramer/George Soros kind of hotel." Max swallowed. "Besides, he wants to get into this party. The chef outdid himself with the food. These miniature lobster *vol au vents* are to die for."

Max might be more right than he knew. "Jesus, Max! There shouldn't be lobster anything at this party! Can you keep them from bringing any more out?" Joshua begged.

"Probably not." Did Max have no sense of urgency? "Things are in full swing."

Oh fuck. Craig was walking into a death trap. "Try, Max. And try to find Craig, and, ah, don't touch him with your lobster hands, okay?"

"You're making it sound like a matter of life and death. It's food." Max spoke around another mouthful.

"It's a matter of life and death all right!" Joshua half-shouted. "He's allergic, this could kill him!"

"I'll try, Josh, but this place is a sea of monkey suits. Can't you text him?"

"I did." His phone still hadn't chimed with an acknowledgement. "I'll try again."

Joshua stabbed at the screen. His message autocorrected into garble. He tried again, typing something more like a warning, but... what if Craig's phone was turned low? Or off? Or—he might be struggling to breathe even now. He tried calling on voice and got nothing but a request to leave a message.

Joshua could barely get the words out through his tight throat. "Craig, don't go into the party. They're serving lobster. Call me back, text me, let me know you got this!" He hung up. Would his messages go through in time?

The seconds ticked away with each thump of his heart. Every beat brought Craig closer to a table loaded with delicious death.

No time to wait—and he had another way.

"Gotta go. Mind the desk." Joshua ripped open the concierge's storage room. Yes! Both bikes had come back from their afternoon jaunt around Manhattan. He wheeled the ten-speed past Lauren. "I wouldn't do this if it wasn't important."

Managing to ram Henry in the side with a handlebar, Joshua pelted through the revolving door, knowing it was big enough to accommodate the bike. He mounted and brushed by the startled doorman. How fast could he get to the sister hotel?

He pedaled frantically, dodging the pedestrians out for evening strolls to dinner or drinks. Maybe Craig would pick up this time? Or answer a text, just so Joshua would know he was out of the danger zone. At every red light he couldn't outrun, he hit redial. "At the sound of the tone…"

Would he have enough breath to speak if Craig did pick up? His pulse hammered in his ears, maybe hard enough to cover Craig's voice if he did answer.

Joshua pushed harder, faster, his leather-soled shoes rasping against the toothy pedals. He had to get to Craig, and damn all red lights and pedestrians and traffic.

A cab screeched to a halt inches from his leg, the blast of its horn all but knocking Joshua off the saddle. Faster! So what if he didn't belong on the sidewalk, it was less crowded—he could shave minutes, seconds, off his desperate journey.

Every short block ticking by mocked him—he'd never get there in time—he'd be stopped by the lights or murdered by traffic if he didn't keep his wits about him. He zigged west from Park Avenue to Lafayette Street.

Still his journey stretched on. Fifteen minutes might as well be fifteen years.

Every thirty seconds he touched his pocket. Yes, he still had the pen. It hadn't jiggled out to fall in the gutter.

Oh fuck, Max was right about the mess on Barclay Street. Joshua rattled through the wooden pedestrian-way hiding the construction, his teeth clacking and the tires catching at the boardwalk. But there—there! The gleaming glass entryway of the Vivaldi Downtown. Please let him be in time!

Joshua all but threw the bike at the liveried doorman and pelted past him into the lobby. Max's concierge desk lay on the other side of a crowd cluttering up the cream veined marble floor. He charged up to the desk. "Did you find him?"

"No, sorry, and they wouldn't let me page him at the party." Max goggled. Had he never seen a raving maniac across his desk before?

"Then you better get me in there, quick." Where was the Malachite Room? He snapped back and forth, searching for signage hidden by the lavishly dressed guests.

"Um, Josh…" Max hesitated.

"Now!" Joshua barked. "Or do you want a death in your hotel?"

"Um, no…" Max locked down his computer. He led Joshua to a serpentine staircase. "This is faster than the elevator." They dodged society matrons and their be-tuxed companions, charging up the left side of the stairs.

Joshua didn't need a guide once he heard the screaming.

He blazed through the anteroom and into a green-veined banquet room, pushing aside men and women whose protests meant nothing. Not against a high-pitched shriek of "Craig!"

"I've got his meds!"

Oh there—oh my God, there was Craig—was that Craig? With his face red and welted, swollen, his eyes puffed shut? He was down, gasping through engorged, bluish lips. His tongue protruded, fatter than it should be. A woman in silver knelt next to him, dumping her handbag out on the floor. "I thought I had another—"

"I do." Joshua skidded to his knees. Forcing his shaking hands to work, he prepped the pen. He jabbed Craig's thigh right through the trousers, holding still and trying to count ten seconds of eternity.

For long moments Craig's breathing remained a horrible gasp.

Joshua gathered him up against his chest, rocking him. "Keep breathing, Craig!"

"Oh thank God," the woman cried. "I've called 911."

"Might be a while until they get here," someone said.

No, they had to get here with reinforcements! Craig's breathing eased, but this room was allergen city—people held tiny plates of death. "Everyone get back, especially if you've eaten the puff pastry things. Or shrimp. Anything shellfish. Get back, give him air. Back!"

"Joshua," Craig croaked. "Need…"

He needed a hospital, and he needed to get out of here. "What kind of ETA did 911 tell you?" Joshua yelled to the room at large.

"They didn't," the woman answered. "He needs to get away from the buffet."

No ETA—and no more syringes.

"Did he eat anything?" Oh, please don't let Craig have swallowed a mouthful of poison…

"No, just contact," she said, patting at him. "Craig—"

"Don't leave me," Craig croaked against Joshua's chest, more vibration than words.

"I won't," Joshua promised. Not until the paramedics pried Craig out of his arms, but they were allowed, they had more meds. And they weren't here. He had to get Craig away from the lobster, and everyone who kept trying to touch the man with their contaminated hands. "Get a wheelchair!"

And a teleporter—Craig needed help right now, not twenty minutes from now.

They had to get downstairs, where they'd waste a lot of time. Or they could go up.

Because this hotel had the next best thing to Scotty beaming them anywhere. Joshua scrambled for his phone and found the number. A private number he'd spent serious cred to track down two years ago. "Hey, Dennis, how fast can you get a bird to the helipad of the Vivaldi Downtown? I have a guy who needs to get to New York-Pres faster than ASAP."

"You don't want to wait for the paramedics?"

"No, he can't." Joshua checked Craig's breathing again. Too slow, too thin, too choked. "He's in anaphylaxis. He'll die if we don't get him out of here."

"Lemme check." In a twenty-year moment he returned. "Got one of the Sikorskis doing the Statue of Liberty/Ellis Island tourist loop. That's the only pilot I've got. It's Friday night."

Joshua had Craig's credit card. He'd promise anything necessary to keep Craig alive. "He'll comp their flights, okay? Just get that chopper over here, please."

"Okay, gotcha." Dennis turned away, to fill the air with staticky conversation. He returned. "Five minutes. Be up top."

Thank God. Max rolled up with a wheel chair, parting the ocean of babbling onlookers.

"On our way." Joshua tried lifting Craig, who flopped helplessly. *Live, Craig, breathe!*

The woman—Felicity? —helped him drop Craig into the chair, and settled his feet on the pads. "Go!"

Please let her not have lobster hands. Don't make this worse. Joshua prayed Craig's every breath, all the way to the elevator. Max raced beside him, dashing ahead to jab his key card into the slot to call the car. The woman ran with them, falling behind quickly but catching up with shoes in hand.

"You gotta tell me who you called to get a chopper that fast," Max panted on the way to the roof.

"Later." Laying his fingers on Craig's neck, Joshua was only slightly reassured to still feel a pulse. Too fast, too weak. He was breathing, though, a horrible raspy rattle.

Joshua was ready to roar out to the center of the circle marking the chopper's target, but held back, Craig lolling in the chair. The *whupwhupwhup* of rescue sounded in the distance, growing louder. Too slowly. Craig's breathing rattled like death.

The helicopter settled in its target, the rotors whipping in endless circles. A door opened and someone beckoned them on. Joshua blinked away tears of desperation and chopper wind to push Craig fast as he could to the door. Half a dozen hands dragged Craig in.

"Joshua…" Craig gasped. "Stay…"

"I'm coming." Whether the pilot liked it or not. Whether there was another seat or not.

"I'm coming with you!" the woman cried, but there was one seat left and Joshua vaulted into it. He slammed the door on her arguments.

He fumbled the seatbelt into position over Craig's lap and managed his own with only one miss. "We're buckled!"

Please let the pilot waste no nanoseconds getting this bird into the air.

The helicopter's engines revved louder and they left the pad. Nausea roiled in Joshua's guts. He pulled Craig to flop against his chest, twisting to hold his stricken friend with both arms. "You're going to be okay, you're going to be okay," he repeated, over and over into Craig's hair, willing it to be true. "We're taking you to the hospital, we're on the way to the ER, I'm with you…"

They barely cleared the tops of the buildings, rushing toward help with a background of patter from the pilot—"We're headed toward the scenic New York Presbyterian Hospital, where we'll touch down in another moment or so"—and stupid comments from the passengers, all "Ooh, like in NCIS or Hawaii 5-0!" Couldn't they just shut up? They were using oxygen Craig needed.

They landed after a quick eternity in the air. Helping hands flung the helicopter's doors open. "Let us have him, sir." They pulled Joshua out as much as he vaulted out of rescue's way. Craig looked so swollen. So still.

"He has a severe allergy to shellfish, someone probably kissed him after eating lobster," Joshua babbled.

Competent hands pulled Craig away from the chopper in a flurry of "We hope your husband's okay!"

Hope wasn't enough, Craig needed more treatment. "I stuck him in the thigh with his EpiPen."

"When?"

"Uh, about ten minutes ago?" Joshua guessed. It seemed like years.

They laid him out on a gurney, some strapping him down, others holding a mask to his face. Oxygen, Craig needed oxygen.

"One mil epi nebs, and stick him again," someone barked. A lot of things happened all at once, half on the run.

"Stay with me," Craig gasped.

"I'm here." Craig wanted him there, needed him there. Joshua grasped Craig's hand, trotting beside the gurney. Craig had a grip now, he had muscle tone, things were getting better already.

The elevator rang with O2 sats and blood pressure, pulses and other jargon Joshua didn't understand, but Craig had lost that red look, and even before they reached the ER level, his lips seemed less puffy through the clear mask. His eyes opened to slits.

"Let us have him now," one of the nurses instructed him. "We'll come get you, but we need you to fill out the paperwork."

"I'll be here," he assured Craig with a last hand squeeze, and tried not to scream when they disappeared through swinging doors.

Somehow he managed to fill in enough of the blanks to satisfy the ward clerk, and if he didn't have insurance information, he had the number to a double-platinum credit card. The means to an end, if it got Craig the treatment he needed.

An hour passed, an hour of pacing and fretting. Of nearly shitting himself from the fear and not wanting to find a lavatory because that would be exactly when someone would come to find him. An hour longer than even the minutes after he'd stabbed Craig like he knew what he was doing. *Please let Craig be okay.*

Finally, someone called him. Or maybe she didn't call him, but she meant him. Because if a nurse called for "Mr. Ridley" out here, he'd answer. To get to the Mr. Ridley in there.

"Yes?" Joshua didn't quite run to her side. "How is he?"

"Your husband's much better already, Mr. Ridley. He's sitting up and asking for you." She ushered Joshua back through exam rooms defined by drapes, ringing with weeping and cries of "Oh Gawd!" and "Fuck!" that nearly drowned out wailed prayers and rapid-fire requests for gauze pads and drugs. "You saved his life, you know."

Joshua pushed through the swinging draperies to find Craig closer to upright than he'd been since he'd left in the Rolls. He was festooned with IV lines and a breathing mask, other nameless medical things. His tux jacket had disappeared, his fine shirt was rumpled and missing half the studs and one sleeve, and who knew where his bow tie had gotten to, but who cared? Craig was a healthy pink, his eyes were back, and he could smile through lips that were still too full.

The head of the bed was raised, and if Craig wasn't able to get up on his own, he didn't have to. Before he said more than "Josh—" and lifted his hands, Joshua was on him, bent to hug and maybe weep.

With lips against Craig's forehead and arms around the man he'd never truly touched, Joshua shook with relief. "You're okay."

Craig hugged him back. "Thanks to you. You were there when I needed you."

Always, Joshua wanted to promise. Always.

Chapter Fourteen

The nurses flitted in and out for another two hours, monitoring Craig's vital signs, ignoring that Joshua had pulled up a chair bedside and kept Craig's hand pressed against his face. Words were too clumsy for their relief.

"There's a risk of a secondary reaction, but since you're stable now and you both know what to do, I don't think we need to admit you tonight," the doctor told them around two a.m. "Since you have a levelheaded caregiver, we can send you home with oral meds and another pen, if you're feeling up to it."

Craig glanced around, locating his tuxedo jacket hanging off an IV pole. "I really want to get out of here and sleep for a week." He yawned. "There's a very comfortable bed waiting."

"I'll take him home," Joshua added. If Craig was well enough to leave and wanted to, that's what he'd get. If "home" didn't exactly include Joshua, no sense mentioning it to the doctor.

Craig suffered the wheelchair ride to the emergency room door but wobbled when allowed to his feet on the sidewalk. Joshua wrapped one arm around Craig's shoulders. He didn't quite fit into Joshua's armpit but made up for it with an arm around Joshua's waist. For stability. Yeah. Only for that, because he couldn't get too used to contact with a man who'd probably ask him to change his plane ticket to Sunday and still leave. At least Craig could leave on his own two feet.

Joshua stuck his other arm out, waving at the taxis trolling by. "We'll be back in about twelve minutes, if I can get one of these taxis to stop for us." Too many had their lights off, but one pulled up to drop its passengers, a woman holding a crying child.

Joshua bundled Craig into the back seat before anyone else could lunge. The short trip back to midtown had Craig's head on Joshua's shoulder. The dark streaked with headlights and tail lights: the city never slept but did slow down. Enough not to need crazy turns and sudden accelerations through stop lights, not enough to pretend this was a romantic jaunt.

Still felt really right. And much too temporary.

The cab pulled up beneath the port cochère, where earlier the Silver Wraith had collected Craig for disaster. Joshua tried to slide out. "Wait here, Craig. I'll get a wheelchair."

"No, it's okay. I can walk," Craig insisted. "I'm fine."

Craig didn't look fine at all, but he was counting out bills into the cabbie's hand and making the numbers add up correctly. Should he take this as a sign Craig knew his reactions best? Or as bravado and guts?

It wouldn't matter either way, if Craig stepped out of the van and fell on his face. Joshua zipped around to Craig's side of the cab for support.

Poor guy felt like noodles cooked past *al dente*. He clung to Joshua, one arm hooked over a shoulder. "Don't even think about it. Just get me upstairs, okay?" Craig managed to greet the night doorman, which got them through the revolving door. They probably looked like a couple of lushes, not that drunks were such a novelty at a posh hotel.

The overnight concierge had the desk when Joshua guided Craig into the lobby. Henry was nowhere to be seen, but Nick made a beeline for them. Of course he'd head off any undesirables that made it past the doorman. His eyes widened, and he was way too full of questions.

Like, "Where have you been?"

Nick may have moderated his language in front of a guest, but Joshua heard *Where the hell* quite plainly. "Emergency room. Penthouse guest had a medical emergency and came close to dying. He's okay now." Joshua hitched Craig a little more upright with some stealthy hip action.

"Right. More like getting plastered together at some bar that likes to comp drinks to the *daylight people*," Nick snapped.

The elevator was only a little farther...

Nick left off his full volume bitching but followed, hissing, "You could have called, instead of disappearing half your shift."

"Sorry. Had other things to think about." He'd have some 'splaining to do, no doubt, but a living, breathing guest had to be worth some slack to management. Even if he was staggering and had a poor chance of staying upright alone. "Lauren knew why I took off, I'm sure she filled you in. Our guest is still feeling pretty rocky and needs to get to bed."

"Where you will no doubt take extra good care of him."

"Back off," Craig snapped. "You're not helping."

Nick stomped back to the desk, his footsteps ringing against the marble. The elevator car opened, disgorging a crowd of designer-dressed partiers, all of whom staggered nearly as badly as Craig and undoubtedly had a better time achieving their rubber legs. Joshua hit a button randomly and used the voyage skyward to rifle Craig's pockets for his keycard.

Craig managed to turn so Joshua had access to the correct pocket. "How'd you convince the hospital you're my husband?"

A pity they weren't on groping terms or in groping condition: a better opportunity for a little closed-chamber grab-ass would never arise.

"I didn't, really." The door opened to an empty hallway on the forty-second floor. Joshua used the keycard to send them the rest of the way to the penthouse. "The people in the chopper assumed it, the emergency staff went with it, and I didn't tell anyone different." He guided them through the door and across the plush carpeting to the master bedroom. "I knew your date of birth and allergies, and had access to your credit card. They didn't question."

He parked Craig on the edge of the bed, where he stayed upright and even shed his own jacket and undid studs on his shirt. Joshua knelt to remove shoes and socks, and retrieve a cufflink that spun from Craig's fingers. "Lovely vintage piece." He ran a thumb over the engraved initials. "Looks like late fifties?"

"I think so." Craig managed to set the cufflink's twin on the bedside table. "My grandfather's. Uh, you knew my birthday?"

Heat grew under Joshua's collar. "Yes."

That got a chuckle, and a hand on his shoulder. For balance. Of course.

"Why?"

Might as well blurt it out. "I checked you out online before deciding to head upstairs that first night. Figured any ax-murdering tendencies might show up before I found out the hard way. It was on your Wikipedia page."

"Is that all?" Heavy though Craig's eyelids drooped, he still looked arch.

No, there was the truth Joshua hadn't admitted. "And I wanted to know more about you."

This was not the conversation he wanted to have with a man whose trousers he would need to help remove for no romantic purposes at all.

"This isn't quite fair. You don't have a Wikipedia page." Braced against Joshua, Craig levered himself to his feet. He waited until Joshua rose before undoing his trousers and stepping out of them. "So, by doing a superior concierge job, you convinced them."

"They drew some conclusions. I didn't correct them." Joshua walked Craig to the bathroom, not knowing how he was going to preserve either of their dignities once they arrived at the plumbing. "It would only muddy the waters."

"The waters are plenty muddy," Craig agreed, reaching for his toothbrush. "Might do with some clarity about what we are to each other. Since I'm saying yes and your reasons for no don't sound like you don't want me."

He'd bid Craig farewell yesterday, or the day before, hadn't he? How could they be anything at all to each other? Yet— he'd blown out of the hotel like a cat on fire to reach Craig when he only suspected a problem. "What do you want us to be to each other?"

Craig reached for his toothbrush, and left it suspended inches away from the toothpaste while he met Joshua's eyes in the mirror. "What I wish for is that we could be two men who just happened to meet through some goofy rent-a-friend arrangement and got to know each other better. And were just... men." He turned to lean a hip against the marble vanity, meeting Joshua's eyes. "Who could be lovers, if they wanted to. But there's all the things in the way that you've already pointed out. Distance. Time." He set the toothpaste down but his knuckles whitened around the purple handle of his toothbrush. "Money even, though it's a tool, not a virtue or..."

Joshua had to clear the lump out of his throat, a gesture that flickered in dozens of reflections. "You only needed money for the things that weren't us. For stuff. But not... Money had nothing to do with why I came upstairs with a deck of cards." That was for pride. The first time. "And it had nothing at all to do with why I came back."

"There's that at least." Craig guided the brush toward his mouth and missed. He let the brush flop down, oblivious to the aqua smear on his cheek. "Would you have done the mad dash across town for any of your clients?"

"No." Joshua wanted to thumb away the peppermint streak. Or kiss it away. "I would have sent the bellman. And it would have been too late for that stranger. I did it myself for you."

"Thank you." Craig's smile moved only one corner of his mouth. Or maybe that was the last of the anaphylactic puffiness. "I just wish that changed anything else about us that would make a difference."

Could he do anything, promise anything, that would lift Craig's defeated shoulders? Would holding him close be more than a horrible tease and a travesty?

Craig found some resolve inside that straightened him up. A totally fine sight in nothing but the clinging blue boxer briefs, with his well-toned chest in its light dusting of hair. Nothing Joshua should be looking at—it was only torture.

Craig pointed. "Now out. I can manage." He stuck the brush into his mouth and began to scrub, turning away from Joshua in what felt like a very final way.

"Are you sure?" Joshua's heart sank. The last thing they needed was Craig hitting his head on a fixture on his way down. A second ER visit tonight would....

But not only did Craig manage to scrub his teeth without falling, no hideous thumps sounded from behind the door he managed to shut in Joshua's face.

In fact, Craig was steady, if slow, on his way to the bed. He didn't really need Joshua holding the covers up so he could slide under the duvet.

Joshua lifted them anyway. Better to get him covered, because the sight of this tantalizing man clad in nothing but some silky underwear might just make him lose his resolve. He tucked Craig in and turned to hide his reaction. Hanging the tux in the closet gave him a chance to control himself.

"Thanks." Craig lay on his back, his dark hair wisping out against the luxurious pima pillowcase, everything from the neck down hidden away. "I have no right to ask this, but, Joshua? Would you stay, please? The meds make me woozy and tired, and—"

"And you really shouldn't be alone." He'd known he'd face this temptation the minute the doctor released Craig—he'd been discharged only because Joshua looked competent. And there was no way he could detect anything wrong from the second bedroom.

"Yeah." Craig's eyes were closer to being his eyes again than they were on the way out of the hospital, and his mouth was only a little puffy. As if he'd spent a long time kissing like he meant it. "But... could you maintain the illusion of being my husband for another few hours? Until I have to catch a plane?"

"How much of an illusion?" Joshua's heart beat a little faster. A taste of what he might have had?

"Not that." Craig shrugged. "But stay with me? I'm going to take another Benadryl, just in case, and it'll knock me for a loop. I don't usually have secondary reactions, but... I'm a wreck, I feel like crap, and I don't want to be alone. Just—be close enough to touch?"

He'd come this far. "What do I do if you have a secondary reaction?"

"Stick me again, if I can't stick myself." The new EpiPen lay next to the cufflinks on the bedside table. "I know it's not fair to ask."

"Doesn't matter. You need me, and I'm here." *And I've wanted to be in bed with you from the start.* "Give me a couple of minutes in the shower. I smell like hospital and fear."

He wanted to drag out his shower, enjoy taking the edge off, the edge he didn't dare bring to bed. Instead

Joshua went for max thrust, minimum time, and still getting clean. He emerged from the bathroom clad in his underwear, to find Craig asleep on his side, his dark locks joining with the shadows on the pillow.

Joshua hit the lights and slid in behind Craig. Had to make sure he was still breathing. Yeah, that's why Joshua snuggled up close and wrapped his arm around the man he couldn't have.

Chapter Fifteen

The unfamiliar pressure on his chest brought Craig swimming to consciousness. Where was he? When was he? And who...?

The darkness of a strange room lit only with the glow from the digital clock and the crisp whisper of the sheets, oh yeah. Wee hours, hotel, but... Craig never woke up next to strangers. Never.

Even as he rolled to his back without disturbing his companion, the knowledge flooded back. This was no stranger—this was the man he'd spent his New York evenings with. Light from the clock was enough to paint shadows on a face he'd not seen so closely. Eyes closed, his lashes making dark lace, Joshua breathed evenly, his exhalations warm on Craig's jaw.

Close enough to kiss.

Still a million miles away. Even with his arm curved around Craig's chest.

But he'd been close when it really counted. Craig hated the memories of gasping for breath around a tongue swollen too large for his mouth. Of losing sight of the world while his eyelids grew too huge to open. Of struggling to breathe through a throat nearly closed. Of fighting the nausea that would finish choking him if his gorge rose completely. Of feeling a hint of relief after Felicity stuck him, and the helplessness of that not being enough. Of her hesitating because she thought he'd stick himself, and his pocket turned up empty.

Thank God for Joshua. Who'd said *No, no, no,* until he'd appeared like an angel because *Yes* was in there somewhere.

He sucked in great gouts of air, because he could. Because he'd come so close to not being able to fill his lungs.

Every breath was a treasure. Every breath scented with Joshua's skin was a greater treasure, the kind that couldn't be bought. The kind that might never be repeated. Craig inhaled again, savoring what he could of his companion. Joshua smelled of life and possibilities. When he woke Craig would find out what those possibilities were. And for now—Craig breathed.

He reached up to rest his hand on Joshua's forearm. The hairs tickled his palm as he eased skin against skin. He wouldn't wake his companion—his night had been as bad as Craig's own, if in a different way. But this much should be okay. Even if he wanted more than anything to lean the inch to Joshua's lips.

He wouldn't disturb Joshua by taking more than he'd been offered when they were both awake. That would have to wait until this maddening, amazing man could either draw back or lunge forward. But this much he'd treasure, and he could hope for more.

The drugs might have saved Craig but they hadn't left his system. The antihistamines weighed down his eyelids, and Joshua's even breathing sang a lullaby he couldn't resist. The softest flutter of air caressed Craig's lips, and he sank back into sleep. Lying in Joshua's arms felt safe.

Have to find a way to make it last.

Chapter Sixteen

Joshua woke snuggled up next to the man he'd been dreaming about. All his resignation about nothing happening between them had gone up like so much smoke when Craig asked him to stay. Maybe nothing had happened, but somehow everything had changed.

Peeling himself stealthily from his companion, Joshua worked his way to the edge of the bed. Was his toothbrush still in the other bathroom? He should clean up and get out, before he put Craig on the spot about what came next. Or before Craig could ask the awkward questions Joshua still had no good answer to.

He should dress. Button his shirt, tuck in the tails, and slide the suit coat over his shoulders. Maybe not slip away like a shadow before Craig woke, but withdraw to the sitting room until he stirred. Joshua could risk waiting at some decent distance now; Craig wasn't in imminent danger of puffing up again. Thank God. His eyes bore only faint traces of the hideous swelling from last night, and his mouth was back to looking entirely too kissable.

Joshua bolted for the far bathroom before he bent down to find out for himself.

Fortified with toothpaste, razor, and resolve, Joshua considered abandoning his clothing until Craig was up and about and had put something on. He wouldn't stick to the leather couch too badly.

Just badly enough. Joshua could retrieve the New York Times from just outside the suite's door and read it at the table, where the brocade chair couldn't do worse than leave woven patterns on the backs of his thighs.

Except that meant opening the door and letting a bit of the world in. If he was going to detach himself from the fine Corinthian flytrap, he'd go check on Craig.

Joshua's gut rumbled. Yesterday's lunch might have been a thousand years ago, and Craig's dinner had been rudely interrupted by a medical emergency. He'd be ravenous. The number for the closest vegetarian restaurant was in his phone list...in the other room.

Though he wasn't willing to run and fetch. Good thing he wasn't the only concierge in this hotel.

Hmm, maybe he hadn't been as stealthy as he thought. Joshua made his call from the side of an empty bed. He stumbled over the order, because Lauren recognized his voice.

"Is kosher towel guy okay, Josh?" The concern in her voice had a lot of overt curiosity in it. "Are you okay?"

"Fine, Lauren, he's fine. Hungry." He didn't want to discuss degrees of fineness. "Just send someone to Twenty-Four Carrots for two egg biscuits and two cups of fruit." Should he specify "someone who isn't Henry?"

Oh, wait. Saturday morning was as assuredly a Henry-free time as it was a "kosher-restaurant free" time. The action would be more lucrative come evening, and Henry didn't miss a dollar.

Lauren laughed. "He must be very hungry indeed."

Oh good, she didn't immediately assume the second serving was for him. No sense in telling her anything she'd need to disavow later. "Give him a break, he hasn't eaten since yesterday noon, and it's nearly lunchtime now." Neither had Joshua. Maybe the jet engine rumble from his belly didn't carry through the phone. He ended the call on another round of gut-grumbles.

Singing in wonderful tone and no known key cut off when Joshua peeked through the bathroom door into a cloud of soap-scented steam. To check on fineness. Could anyone that far out of tune be truly healthy? Craig stepped out of the shower looking good enough to eat with drips running over his skin. He disappeared into the oversized bath towel, only to reappear grinning. The mirrors on all surfaces reflected a thousand angles of gorgeousness with a semi-erect cock.

Joshua swallowed hard. He was lost. Lost as hard as he'd feared he would be when he'd said, "No, we can't." They still couldn't. What the hell were they going to do now?

"Good morning." Craig rubbed his hair to a damp tousle and corrected himself while peeling away the gauze taped to the inner surface of his forearm. The IV puncture showed dark against pale skin. "Fabulous morning."

"Yes, it is." Except for it being a short morning—Craig had an outbound flight today. "You're feeling good?"

"Damn skippy. Better than I expected." He flung the towel over the rack with just enough overlap to keep it from sliding off. "Maybe it was the company in the night. In fact" —he stepped in close enough to ghost the words across Joshua's shoulder—"let's go back to bed."

Back to bed. Where they couldn't go once if he expected to ever get out again. He'd been asked, at last. When the answer couldn't be anything but no if he didn't want to tear his heart out of his chest with his own bare hands.

"When do you need to be at the airport?" Joshua dared not look down at what was almost brushing his hip, or there wouldn't be any point to words.

Craig lifted one eyebrow. "Tomorrow. If you're off tomorrow, then Monday. Or if you can take some vacation at no notice, the day you go back. How long do you have, and what will you show me of your fair home city? I hear there's culture stuff a cow-town boy ought to see."

New York with Craig? Where to even start? All the wonders New Yorkers took for granted? Or prided themselves on not visiting, because tourists flocked there? A day or two or a week would barely scratch the surface. No—he'd offer things only a native would know about. Maybe start with the Whispering Gallery at Grand Central Station? No, not yet, Joshua needed some time to arrange for a string quartet at the station, or was that too sappy? To hell with sappy—it was too close to an oyster bar and Craig didn't need another medical adventure. Note to self, stay out of Grand Central... Maybe a stroll down to the Waldorf-Astoria for a look at Cole Porter's piano, on the way to the Burns Collection. He'd have to give Dr. Burns a call, let him know they were coming, surely Doc would let them in of a Saturday, it was for Joshua after all...

Craig cleared his throat. "You said you had Saturday off. Spend it with me. I can change the flight."

Whoops, Joshua'd paused too long, even though he was dithering and not refusing. "I do, but just Saturday. I can fix your flight. I should…"

"No, no, really, I can do things for myself. Or for us. I'm not leaving." Craig grabbed his phone from the bedside table. His gut rumbled hard enough for Joshua to feel it at two paces.

"See how I'm changing my flight?" Craig spared a glare for the canned announcements and hold music wafting from his phone. "If they don't have a seat on the same flight, there's the red-eye, or Monday early. While you're at work I could investigate who's buried in Grant's Tomb."

"Nobody. They're entombed above ground," Joshua mumbled. Craig was changing his reservations? Or more likely, buying a whole new ticket? To stay another day? With him? Didn't the man remember he had a business to run? Oh okay, the business would probably survive a day or three without Craig's oversight, but…

"Good to know." Craig grinned, the phone to his ear. Maybe the airline knew they were keeping a very important person on hold, or Craig had a special number, because his attention turned to "Hello, I need to change my return on flight 3652 from today until tomorrow. Yes, great…"

If it was a special VIP phone number, Joshua would need to get it. In the meantime, a man staying another night needed a place to lay his head. Otherwise Craig would need to be out of here by noon, and forget that, the day was theirs. Joshua sat at the edge of the bed and punched a single digit on the phone. Best to tailor his carrots and sticks to the specific front desk associate. What worked on Tyler might make no impression on one of the others.

"Hey, Lauren," Joshua started out. "Who's on the front desk?"

"Why? Something I can't take care of for you?" she asked. "Or for your billionaire boyfriend, since I'm on duty and you're not?"

"You'd manage everything exquisitely." He let the boyfriend crack go—he needed to soothe her. "But this is a front desk thing. Gotta let the poor FDA do their job."

She giggled. "Like selling the penthouse suite at a fraction of the going rate? Tyler got some shit over your pal. Grant had a couple of choice words about that, and you may or may not have been thrown under the bus."

Grant might be pissed about it, but the metric crapton of money Joshua made for the hotel left him better equipped than any FDA to weather any resulting storm. "Meh, I'll take the heat. Tyler'll owe me one."

"In case your buddy comes back? Really, Josh, if you read the financial news, you'd know he can afford the suite." She *hmm*'d under her breath, the tap of her keyboard in the background. "SecurNow closed—"

"Lauren!" Joshua wanted to poke his finger through the phone right into her ear. Didn't matter who was on the desk, he could figure out the right pressure on the fly. "Just transfer me. I need to extend Mr. Ridley's stay. He's not up to traveling today."

"I thought you said he was fine?" Lauren pounced.

"Not fine enough to travel," he improvised. "Exhausted."

Not-exhausted Craig was more than fine—he'd finished his call and had crawled across the bedding to hug Joshua from behind, the better to nibble his ear. Oh damn, that... Time to resort to begging. "Please, Lauren, just transfer me over to, it's Scott and McKenna today. Because I can just hang up and call back..."

Thank goodness she let him evade more questions, because the nibbling from behind was getting more and more distracting. At least McKenna didn't ask stupid questions about why he was extending the penthouse reservation or require a sweetener. Tyler might have argued, but with luck, he and problem sweetie were gorging on pumpkin-spiced challah French toast or something equally trendy at Spoons. Double payoff!

Might have been fun to take Craig there himself, but it meant getting dressed and leaving the vicinity of this nice soft bed. Not happening. He couldn't even manage to turn around.

"How long do we have before food shows up?" Craig's nibbling made Joshua's brain short out.

"Um, ten minutes maybe?" Joshua wanted to savor the strong arms around his chest and the hard cock pressed against his back. "If we're fast..."

"I don't do fast." If his lips on the shell of Joshua's ear were anything like they'd be on his cock, ten minutes would be more than adequate. If he'd reach down to the chubby waving around just below his hand, wouldn't take much at all.

"Oh really?" Joshua's head was getting a little swimmy. "How do you like it?"

"Slow. Real slow. There's ways to make it last and last. I want to make you climax half a dozen times before you blow your load." With two fingers Craig swiped a trail of fire up Joshua's neck. "Might not get there this first time, not even close, but the learning curve's fun."

"Is that even possible?" Joshua could turn to look this crazy new lover in the eye, but it was so much nicer to tilt his head for neck-nibbles.

"You bet. But going wild and fast won't get you there." Craig flicked his tongue against the strap muscle. Joshua moaned. "Slow and deliberate, with internal control. Might take a while to learn."

That sounded like—Joshua blinked hard to focus without dislodging Craig from the erogenous zone he'd just located in Joshua's neck. "How long a while?"

"Depends on you," Craig purred. "And our travel schedules. Might be a couple of weeks, might be a couple of months. I think you'll get the hang of it pretty quick."

"How long did it take your last boyfriend?" Had he just agreed to a long-distance relationship? Or slow heartbreak? Or... Did he really want to know the answer to his last question?

"My last boyfriend was in 2011 and is irrelevant to this discussion." Craig lipped at Joshua's earlobe.

"Uh..." Damn but Craig was finding ways to short-circuit his brain. Joshua mumbled, "If you can do that, you'd have guys lined up around the block."

That was enough to make Craig sit back on his haunches and stop nibbling. No cock pressing, no hands on shoulders. "You really don't get it, do you, Joshua?" His tone was sharp, CEO mode, not the purr of a lover. "First I have to meet someone I want to talk to every day. I have to like him as a human being before I even get around to thinking about sex. That happens a lot less often than you'd think. In the meantime, I've learned to amuse myself, which I do extremely well. It keeps me from having to sort through hordes of gold diggers and trophy hunters."

There was a seriously backhanded compliment in there somewhere. Joshua shook his head, trying to dislodge it. "At least you don't think I'm a gold digger. Or a whore."

The fleshy sound of palm meeting forehead made him turn around. Craig ground the heel of his hand into the bridge of his nose, and his erection ratcheted downward.

"No, I don't think you're any of those things. You know that." He took his hand away from his face for a full-on executive stare. "You're amazing company with your clothes on, which means that I want to find out what kind of company you are with your clothes off. Which hasn't happened for me in years."

"I'm... flattered?" Years?

"You should be." Craig hopped off the bed to stand before Joshua in all his naked glory. "The downside of not finding compatible men more often is that my social skills get pretty rusty and you get to see me using only the traits that make me a success in the rest of my life."

He took Joshua's hands and pulled him to standing, and then to embracing. At last. The long sweep of his chest, the muscles in his thighs, his groin, all pressing against Joshua, and the naked appeal in his eyes were too much to resist. Joshua wrapped his arms around this frustrating, amazing man and bent to kiss him. Craig met his mouth softly, a mute appeal to understanding. He let his tongue travel against Joshua's lower lip.

As if he could let go now. He leaned into Craig's mouth, lapping up the promises he knew were temporary. Today. Tonight. Tomorrow morning. He'd take anything he could get before Craig left, no matter how brief. Damn, but he was lost.

Craig didn't close his eyes when he kissed. Was he as desperate as Joshua to glom up every sight, every sound, every touch and taste? Joshua slid his hands into Craig's hair, winding his fingers into the dark, damp strands.

They came up for air, their cocks at full attention. Joshua backed away enough to let them spring up, batting each other, and then crushed tight to Craig's belly. He let his eyes flutter shut this time, trying to drink up every taste and whimper, to touch every inch of skin with his own.

They broke the kiss, and Craig rested his head on Joshua's shoulder. Joshua nuzzled into the mussy hair. Craig was adorable with wethead. "You mean I get to see you being driven and goal-oriented and not accepting anything short of success when it comes to being with me?"

"Sounds about right," Craig agreed. He shifted his grip to rest a hand on the small of Joshua's back. "You're the guy who makes the impossible happen, so maybe you could turn some of that persistence on being with me?"

"I know a guy at Teterboro Airport..." Joshua said slowly. Because being without this man didn't bear thinking about.

"See, I knew you'd find something." Craig kissed him full on. Thoroughly. Joshua gave himself over to the dance of tongues. Bossy guy. Bossy, wonderful guy. Bossy, pain in the ass, make you reconsider everything guy. Bossy, sexy, warm, horny, delicious guy.

Joshua hated pulling away, even for a moment but— "I think we'd better find some trousers or our food will show up while—"

A vaguely familiar woman stood in the doorway. Someone laughed behind her in a crinkle of paper and a flash of red and gray hotel livery. Shouldn't be Henry fetching breakfast and coffee. The fucktard did so much of his extra pillows business on Saturday nights, he wouldn't waste a precious weekend shift on legitimate fetch and carry. Would he? Whoever it was disappeared behind a shut door, but that left this crazed female gaping at the two of them wearing little besides cologne. Joshua clung more tightly to Craig, and Craig clutched back. Displaying their erections wouldn't be a problem in two more seconds, but jamming against each other was Craig's only fig leaf, and Joshua's boxers didn't leave a lot to the imagination. At least they were standing sideways to the door.

"Hello, Felicity." Craig sounded calmer than Joshua could credit. "I don't recall inviting you up."

"Of course you don't. You didn't." Felicity stared wide-eyed at the two of them. "I came up to see how you were doing."

"Fine as can be, obviously." Craig's cheeks flamed but his voice didn't waver. "Go away now. Shoo."

How Craig could banter while Joshua could only stand with his face burning and his balls trying to hide somewhere around his pancreas was a marvel of strength. But Felicity wasn't shooing or scatting or otherwise leaving.

"We have a plane to catch." She averted her eyes at last.

"You have a plane to catch. I've made other arrangements." Craig let go with one arm enough to flip his hand in dismissal, a gesture much friendlier than his tone. "Safe travels. Starting. Right. Now."

"The last time I saw you, you were struggling to breathe," she snapped, still staring at the blank face of the big screen TV, and not, thank goodness, at them.

"I texted you on my way out of the hospital that I was all right." Craig positively crackled with fury. Joshua would let go except he'd probably erupt where he stood. "Now you've seen for yourself that I'm intact and healthy. Yes, I could have notified you that I've changed my plans, and I would have, presently, but you're a big girl and can travel without me. Now go."

"What you texted me" —she resumed staring at them, the better to aim the acid— "was 'I'm oj', which was not particularly reassuring."

"I am 100 percent peachy. And you are leaving."

The defiant harpy in the Jil Sander suit didn't budge.

Craig stopped glaring daggers at Felicity long enough to flick a glance and a soft "Sorry" Joshua's way.

"Now." He jerked away from Joshua to stalk toward their intruder, who didn't spare him a glance. She stared at Craig, who grabbed her upper arm and forcibly turned her to the door. "Good bye, Felicity."

He marched her nearly to the exit before she shook herself loose and ran. Craig watched her go, hands on his hips. A slam that would have rattled a lesser structure became a dull thud. "Don't let the door hit you where the Good Lord split you."

Helpless laughter burbled up from somewhere around

Joshua's navel. Even watching Craig returning couldn't stem the hysteria. "What… the … fuck?"

"My sentiments exactly." Craig paused near the dining table. "I'm really sorry about that. I should have remembered to intercept her. Should have done it when I changed my flight."

Speaking of interceptions—that killed Joshua's crazed mirth. "Just in case…" He whipped through the living room to hang the "Do not disturb" sign on the external door knob. He leaned against the stout door, bracing against the revolting possibility Henry might give the housekeepers a few instructions. He half-expected to hear knuckles against wood. "Housekeeping shouldn't be headed up this way just yet, but we don't need Amaya or Paolina walking in on us either."

Wouldn't they just love to have a snicker at him? Joshua didn't need to hear any more commentary, and neither did Craig. Why couldn't a man just fall in love in peace?

"Good thinking." Craig sniffed his way to the paper bag. He investigated the contents. "More good thinking. Mm, look. Foooooodddd…." He lured Joshua away from his support with a neatly wrapped packet and a cup of mixed berries. "The better to fortify you for when I pounce."

The better to get past the horror of the interruption and quell the growling in their middles. The still-warm scrambled egg and cheese encased in Manhattan's flakiest biscuit might be enough to overwhelm even Felicity's championship-worthy cockblocking.

What kind of life was this, munching takeout breakfast looking down on Manhattan with the morning light turning Central Park into a green jewel flecked with red and gold? With a man who held out a raspberry for Joshua to nibble from his fingertips.

The important part was the raspberry. Because Craig offered it to him. Joshua ate the berry, managing a lipped caress on Craig's fingertips. No raspberry had ever been so tangy or sweet as this one, each drupelet releasing its juice. Because the man who wanted to be his lover fed him.

He offered a strawberry in return. Craig needed two bites to finish the fruit, ending with a kiss in Joshua's palm. He shivered.

Perhaps he should have ordered two sandwiches for each of them—Craig peeked into the bag for more. Joshua hadn't eaten since lunch yesterday either. "About an hour after sunset I can offer you kosher Chinese food."

That snapped Craig's head up. "You what? You can? Joshua, you may have found the reason to move to New York."

"For General Tso, but not for me?" Joshua dared tease. "Or just not this week?"

"Arggh!" Craig got up to toss the bag into the trash. "I swear I'm going to fold the United States up like an accordion to put Denver and Manhattan adjacent."

"So much for flyover country." Rearranging the earth's topography might be the one thing that would solve their dilemma. Joshua pulled Craig into his lap. "Back to where we were before we were so rudely interrupted. Slow and easy, you said?"

He could do slow and easy. Maybe. Starting with just the parts he could reach with his mouth. Like Craig's chest, and into his armpit. Damn, he smelled good. Over the swell of his pec, and down. Craig's nipple rose, pebbly against his tongue, and the quick intake of breath said

Joshua was on the right track. He teased the bud even harder, leaving his hand resting against Craig's thigh. He wanted slow, he'd get slow. Even if Joshua wanted nothing more than to wrap his fingers around the delectable cock standing to attention inches from his hand.

He could appreciate the torment too—his own cock filled, lifting against Craig's thigh from below. He couldn't move much, but he'd get there. Better to waft a warm breath against damp skin and make Craig shiver and groan.

"Slow enough for you?" Joshua blew again and swiped his tongue over the pink target near his nose.

"Nngghh" probably meant "yes." So did the tight-ening arm around his shoulder and the twist of fingers in his hair.

"You get a four-minute head start into the bedroom." Joshua sucked a rose of color into the soft skin of Craig's upper arm. "Grab whatever you think we're going to need and get into bed. I want you lying there, watching me come through the bedroom door. Coming to get into bed with you, with intentions of fucking your brains out."

"Oh, fuck yes," Craig groaned. He pulled Joshua's head back long enough to plunder his mouth.

So, boss man liked being bossed. What else did he like? "Unless you wanted to top?"

"Some other time." He shuddered hard. "I want you to fuck me. Damn, I'm getting P-waves just talking about it."

"What are those?" Anything Joshua gave, he needed to understand.

"Contractions in my prostate. Tantric thing." Each word sounded like Craig had to reboot his brain.

Okay, P-waves needed investigation, but not right this minute. All Joshua needed to know was they were good. Maybe even as good as watching Craig head to the bedroom. The man had a nice ass and he'd just invited Joshua to play. Which—damn. Every part of him looked good.

Trying to wait four minutes might kill him. Knowing that Craig was in the bedroom, getting ready. Joshua trailed fingers over his skin, going slow up and down his torso. Like a pendulum, counting off the seconds until he could go in. He didn't dare flick a nipple or cup his balls— the waiting had him wound up. He used up seven seconds sliding his boxers to the floor.

Maybe Craig was on to something with the delayed gratification. But enough with the "delayed."

Four minutes had to have passed. Joshua ambled to the bedroom door, wanting to run. He paused to display himself in the doorway, leaning against the door jamb to survey the fine sight in the bed. Craig lay propped on one elbow, the sheet covering everything to his waist but the outline of his erection. Damn, his smile…

Birdsong warbled from the side chair where Joshua's trousers lay.

"Someone's been blowing your phone up. The stupid thing's been twittering like a whole damn flock." Craig lost the sultry look to glare at the chair.

"I'll make it stop." Joshua would give every speck of attention to Craig and nobody else. He poked the ringer to silence and dropped the device onto the bedside table. It went quiet, the perfect soundtrack for dropping onto the bed and leaning over to kiss the vision awaiting him.

Rolling to his back, Craig held out his arms for Joshua to sink into. How had he ever imagined saying no to this man?

The phone buzzed angrily against the hardwood. Without breaking their kiss, Joshua kicked the phone to the floor. Barely a thump registered, and the carpet muffled the vibration.

Slow, yeah. Lazy explorations of Craig's face with his lips, and the trail of his new lover's fingertips up and down his back. Best Saturday morning ever. Maybe Joshua didn't know a thing about multiple climaxes and the mysterious what-not Craig mentioned, but tracing the ridges of Craig's brows and the straight line of his nose would take lots of time. Craig whimpered deep in his throat when he tried scooting against Joshua's body, and Joshua kept him pinned.

"Time enough for that," Joshua breathed into Craig's ear. He wanted slow, Joshua could do slow. Might kill him not to frot until they blew, but anything this man wanted, he could have. Joshua'd make sure of it.

Except silence, apparently, because the persistent whir from the floor turned into a computer-generated guitar blues riff on the other side of the bed.

"Ignore it," Craig advised, but it went on, and on, until Joshua was ready to fling the damned thing down the elevator shaft.

"Fuck." Craig squirmed out from under Joshua. "Be quiet." He stabbed the screen. "Hmm. It's your GM."

"What? It's my day off." Shithead Grant could take a flying leap off the fifty-second floor of the Vivaldi, because they weren't allowing him up to the fifty-third floor. "Why would he call you, anyway?"

"I chewed him a new asshole yesterday." Craig glared at the ringing phone.

"If he wants you to vacate the suite…" Grant better not countermand what Joshua's persuasion had accomplished at the front desk!

"I think I'll chew him another one." Craig stroked the screen, not lifting it to his ear. "What?"

The answer came through loudly enough for Joshua to hear. "Mr. Ridley, so sorry to bother you—" Bastard didn't sound sorry at all. "—but this is Grant Wetzel, the general manager here at the Vivaldi, and I'd hoped you could help me locate an employee who was last seen with you. Joshua Hannes, the concierge."

"Does the man not get a day off?" Craig snapped.

"Lots of them. Once I notify him he's been fired."

Chapter Seventeen

"What?!" was a joint screech.

"Oh, there you are, Joshua." Smugness dripped out of the slender device in Craig's hand. "Apparently you are indeed with a hotel guest, and I don't want to know if you're still as naked as was reported."

"Fucking Henry," Joshua hissed between his teeth. "That *was* him!"

Craig would fix this. He clapped the device against his head. "This is Craig Ridley, and your concierge has been nothing but professional in his dealings with me. What the hell would you fire him for?"

"I have to discuss that with the employee, Mr. Ridley" was a smooth deflection.

Craig glanced at Joshua, who'd gone pale. "He can tell us both."

Craig held out the phone between them.

"Very well, since you've authorized Mr. Ridley to know, you abandoned your post last night at the busiest time of the evening, you've been repeatedly absent from your desk during the last week to go spend time in the penthouse, and housekeeping reports your clothing has been left in the penthouse all week long. Those ties are quite distinctive." The GM totted off truths that only half explained the situation.

"He abandoned his post to save my life, Wetzel," Craig snarled. "Everything else you've mentioned has been in terms of offering fine service to a guest."

Joshua breathed shallowly, an *oh shit* working his lips.

"Perhaps that service has been a little too fine, then, because the only charges on your concierge account are for meals and theater tickets. Services too private for hotel billing that require nudity, with or without overnight stays, violate New York laws, and are expressly forbidden by hotel policy." The GM paused. "Since you're on hotel property, Joshua, you can have your desk cleared out by noon, you will pick up your final check, and then leave. Your services are no longer required by the Vivaldi Central Park. Nor will you be eligible for rehire, a fact I will mention to anyone calling regarding references. Good day, Mr. Hannes. Enjoy your stay, Mr. Ridley."

Foul words became empty air.

Craig stared at Joshua. "He has no right to do that."

"But he did." Joshua stared down at his clenched fists. "Damn it. It all looks bad and none of it was! Damn it all!" He was up and raging, covering all the carpet in the master bedroom. "I can't believe he made everything out to be so ugly! He didn't listen, he…"

"I can fix this, Joshua." Craig pulled his feet back to sit cross legged on the bed. Joshua wasn't listening to him yet—too caught in the fury. Craig would intervene if Joshua looked like punching walls or furniture, but his rage went to pacing and yelling, with a side of fist shaking. Not that Grant and Henry hadn't earned punches in the mouth, but that wasn't the hardest they could be hit. When the first storm seemed close to burning out, Craig repeated, "I can fix this."

He would, no matter what it cost him, because Joshua had done nothing but good and kindness. No matter what Joshua wanted to come of this, Craig would make it so.

The tall, nude, and utterly wrecked figure of the man who wasn't yet his lover plopped onto the edge of the bed, his head in his hands. "I don't know how. Nothing you said made a difference."

"I have other ways to make myself heard." Craig dared to drape an arm over Joshua's shoulders. "I can't fix the interpersonal stuff between you and that jackass Wetzel, or you and Henry, but... Do you want your job back? I can make it happen."

"I want my life back," Joshua rubbed the heels of his hands against his eyes. "The way it was an hour ago, with all of New York open to me. I could have moved to the Marcel or the Plaza right up until he said no rehire. Now I have a bunch of specialized skills and nowhere to use them."

"You will. I'll make sure of it." Joshua couldn't lose his profession for Craig, though—and he had more resources than he knew, but how to say it? What had gotten results last night? "You do have a wealthy husband."

"That was for the hospital," Joshua snorted. "It's not real."

No, damn it, it wasn't. Yet. "It could be."

"Please, Craig, we were just on the start of a long-distance relationship." Joshua gave him a cock-eyed, what the fuck glare. "Not... Well, guess my life is blown up now."

"That's not what I meant," Craig snapped, jerking his arm back. "You have me as an ally, a friend, and yes, a lover, who has a metric fuckton of money and connections. I am not going to be your 'oh well, might as well' last resort."

Joshua pulled away too. "Didn't say you were. But my career just went down the shitter."

It had. Because of Craig. But snarling at Joshua would-n't improve the "wanting Craig in his life" quotient. "I will fix this for you, for any definition of 'fixed' you have that doesn't involve making your enemies love you," he continued more softly. "I will fix it so they can't bother you, and as for the rest, well, you have to decide what you want. I'll make it happen."

Please let Joshua decide what he wants is to be with me. Even if it is in New York.

The white-hot rage burnt through Joshua, leaving him a shell of himself. Had he managed to alienate Craig too? Especially after the "wealthy husband" crack.

What did he want? Damn it, Joshua wanted it all and there wasn't any way to have it all now, any more than it was possible this morning before everything went to hell.

What he wanted was to be the best damn concierge in New York City.

He couldn't be if he left something undone.

His last act as concierge would not be to stiff the guy who'd done him a favor. "I'm about to spend some more of your money, Craig. Or rather, pay what I promised."

Almost too weary to dial, he punched up access to the hotel system. If Asshat Wetzel hadn't locked him out yet, he could take care of their obligations.

"Who do I owe and how much?" Craig untangled his legs and reorganized thigh to thigh against Joshua. "Oh, yeah, the helicopter. Add another thousand bucks as a tip, okay? I like breathing."

"I will." Joshua leaned into Craig, tapping numbers on the screen. "There. It'll keep Dennis's memory of me green."

Like it mattered now. "Good. You'll still need his good will." Craig kissed the side of Joshua's head, then slid around to straddle his thighs. He cupped Joshua's face and held his gaze.

Not that Joshua could look away. *Anything I want, huh? How about the impossible? Or does that just take a little longer?*

"I appreciate the thought, Craig, but reality looks a little different." Maybe being a kept man wouldn't be so bad. A pride-ectomy might come with good brandy for anesthesia. He could call downstairs for a bottle of Remy Martin and get started...

"I told you, all you have to decide is what you want. Because I already started raining fire down on your asshole of a GM." Craig punctuated that shocker with a kiss to Joshua's nose. "Beginning yesterday, and it's about to accelerate. Once I know which tack you want me to take."

Oh, for fuck's sake. Wrapping his arms around the man who promised him the world didn't make two contradictory things happen. "I... don't know."

"Yes, you do know." Craig drew back sharply, making his flaccid penis swing against Joshua's thigh. "Don't worry about hurting my feelings."

"It's not that." Joshua leaned his forehead against Craig's chest. "I want things that can't exist together, or at all. I want…"

"Your colleagues' good will is problematic. Your job, okay. Done deal. Me, also done deal, with complications. Because maybe I want a Beechcraft Hawker 650 or a Learjet instead of a Challenger 600. So, anything on your wish list I haven't mentioned?" Craig trailed fingertips up and down Joshua's back, soothing as his words, and less of a hollow joke.

"Running away together and leaving everything else behind? On top of all the rest?" Joshua might as well cry for the moon. Not even a billionaire boyfriend could bring that down from the sky.

"You drive a hard bargain, sir." Craig tightened his arms around Joshua's shoulders. "But one 'run away from it all' coming up."

"Sounds good, Craig." He'd play along with the joke. Everything in that burgundy chocolate voice sounded possible. Except—Joshua jerked up to stare into Craig's eyes. "What do you mean, you already started raining fire?"

Craig laughed, deep and evil. "I scheduled the pit of hell to open up on him come Monday morning. One of the Vivaldi's biggest shareholders is a friend and colleague of mine, and he was not pleased with certain activities around here. Your buddy Grant is due for a dick punch. So is his little minion Henry. I did read that situation right?"

"You did." Hope rose in Joshua's chest for the first time since his stiffy went down. "Go on!"

Again that deep chuckle at close range—Joshua's heart sped to double time. "My buddy, whom I will introduce you to sometime when we fly out to Seattle, was most unhappy when I explained the situation, and he will be even less so when he hears of recent developments. In fact, I think I'll spoil everyone's weekend. Except yours." With a press of lips into Joshua's hair, Craig rose from Joshua's lap.

He punched up a number and greeted a legend like a friend.

What the hell had Joshua stumbled into? This was even less believable than Craig's husband jokes.

Craig leaned against the fluffy pillows and the quilted headboard of the king bed, holding one arm out in invitation to climb aboard like a life raft. With his head on Craig's chest and his arm over a washboard belly, Joshua listened to the battle of the leviathans raging over his head.

It started with pleasantries: "Hey, Bill, remember that situation I was telling you about? Oh, yes, I'm fine actually, it did get a little dicey there, but the concierge I mentioned? He saved my life. And got fired for his trouble, with all sorts of ugly accusations, none true.... Yes, the general manager's a total dickhead, and his number is... Oh yes, I'd be happy to stick around and clarify any details."

The promised pit of hell opened.

Fury at a hundred decibels Joshua understood, and vicious cuts in honeyed tones, but he'd never heard anything like the cold ferocity his erstwhile boss faced. Words like "background checks" and "complete audit" launched like torpedoes over his head, with icy exactitude. Nothing to even touch on his own involvement, until "whistleblower" and his name were coupled.

"Which means you can't fire him without dragging the corporation through the mud, and that is not acceptable" made a direct hit from three thousand miles away.

That pained sound might be Grant shitting his pants. Couldn't happen to a nicer guy.

Another volley of fire from the Pacific Northwest scored a direct hit. "Which means his job is secure, unlike your own," launched a storm of "But, but, but…!"

"However, since feelings are running high, he's going to have a year's leave of absence," Craig suggested, grinning most evilly at Joshua.

That brought an agreement from afar, and more "But, but, buts" from fifty-two stories below.

"No, he did not do anything underhanded. He spent a couple grand on a private air ambulance and escorted me to the ER. Check my account." Craig's smooth baritone rang like steel. "Hell, check with the chopper service."

The garble coming past Craig's ear was mostly wrath mixed with some character defamation, and what sounded like a threat.

"Would you prefer he be on site to help the audits?" Craig suggested. "Or give him a leave of absence at full salary?"

The agreement from downstairs came through as a sob.

Craig listened more than he spoke after that, and he ended the call about five minutes later. With both arms around Joshua, he squeezed tightly.

Joshua squeezed back. The giants had danced, and he had not been crushed.

"I think I got everything on your list," Craig murmured. "Even the running away part."

He had. Joshua's throat swelled. "You did. My God. I didn't think it could be done." He clutched more tightly to the man who'd just moved mountains. For him.

"I was motivated." Craig rubbed his lips into Joshua's hair. "Please say you'll run toward me."

A slow, careful exhalation ruffled the hair on Craig's chest, tickling Joshua's nose with possibilities. "Where else could I want to go?"

Chapter Eighteen

One damn thing after another! If anyone or anything dared interrupt them now, Craig would fling it out the goddam window. Without opening the window. He had Joshua in his arms at last, and nothing, no one, could get between them.

He'd hold Joshua as long as it took to let the relief seep all the way through his awareness and into his bones. Poor guy, he'd just been whipsawed as thoroughly as a man could be; no wonder he was shaking. He couldn't have any idea how hard Craig could play hardball.

He'd use a ball made of cement if that's what it took to make things right, and he'd lob it right at any dumbshit who gave Joshua grief. Turds like Grant and Henry could only dodge so much before the splat.

"It's all right, it's all good," Craig murmured into Joshua's hair. "I have your back." He did. Had to, and not just because he'd painted the target on Joshua.

Wouldn't mention the L-word yet. Not to a man who'd had every other surprise in the world, all bad, thrown at him in the last twenty-four hours. Demonstrating it, though…

And maybe he already had.

Eh, he'd keep going. Soon, because Joshua was clutching him less like a drowning man and more like a lover. Craig breathed shallowly—that flat plane of hipbone and the angle around to his side was a wildly sensitive spot, and Joshua'd wrapped his hand there like he'd been given a map.

"All this for a man you've barely kissed." Joshua rubbed his cheek against Craig's chest, velvety soft.

"Better fix that." Craig toyed with the shell of Joshua's ear, rubbing his lips into the curls of dark hair. "Now that we've got all the bullshit out of the way, no reason not to. Or is there anything else that needs to be vanquished?"

Joshua froze. Craig froze. *What now?*

Joshua softened. "I was going to say, 'my underwear', but they're on the floor." He started to climb up Craig's body, landing with his elbow on the pillow.

"Don't scare me like that." Craig pulled Joshua down on top of him. Nothing but full body contact would do now. The press of skin to skin had to squeeze out all the danger and the fear from between them. All the hesitation. The doubts and the what ifs wouldn't survive the glorious melding of mouths, or the tangle of arms and legs. Craig moaned, opening his mouth under the suddenly fierce onslaught. This man... Oh, Joshua...

Fulfilling all the promise of his personality, even more himself naked and erect than he was on his feet in a suit. Thoughtful—he did more of what Craig moaned for. Resourceful—he squirmed between Craig's thighs without squashing anything precious. Intent—like his whole world was the size of this bed.

"Slow, you said?" Joshua mumbled his way to Craig's neck. With their fingers entwined and their arms spread out, Craig was content to let Joshua drive. He turned his head for all the attention Joshua wanted to lavish on the big strap muscle in his neck. Which, oh fuck, was a lot. With his tongue and his lips and the graze of teeth... And all the time in the world.

Because Joshua understood slow. He understood thorough. Craig tipped his chin higher, the soft *Ahhh...* escaping from between parted lips. He'd have to treat Joshua to an equally extravagant exploration, in a bit... Yeah, in a bit, after... There wasn't any "after", it was all right now, and the caresses they'd told themselves and each other they couldn't have.

Damn if they weren't having it all. Craig squeezed Joshua's hands, rubbing his thumbs up and down from knuckle to well-buffed nail. All he could add to the slow explorations up top. Damn but he was hard, and his cock nestled against Joshua's answering solidity, scraping through the nest of curls at his base in the rise and fall of their bodies.

"Slow enough?" was a hell yes—mouth to mouth slowed them down before Craig could beg for more speed. Joshua tasted of mint and happiness, the crinkles around his eyes betraying his amusement.

"Feels good." Better than what he'd imagined every night so far. Except last night. Last night didn't bear thinking on—he was alive and breathing, even if he was a bit squashed.

Drawing featherlight fingertips up and down Joshua's spine made him shiver and laugh. "That's..." Joshua shivered again.

"Too much?" Pressing his palms against skin would still the shivers. "I'll stop."

"Don't stop, but, different?" Joshua shivered again. "Or it's too tickly."

"Not tickly, got it." Oh the joys of learning a man who knew what he liked and could say so. Longs sweeps of palm would still the tickles, responding with the play of muscles beneath skin. "You feel so good."

"So do you." Joshua went back to finding out just how good it felt. Craig would give him an hour to stop. Hell, he'd give him two hours to stop that, or three hours, or four. A lifetime.

How had he become so lost? Yet he was found. Because Joshua was touching him as if he had done it for a thousand years and would do it for another thousand years.

With hands and mouth alone he could bring Craig off, if Craig would relax enough to allow it. Even exploring nothing below Craig's clavicle, Joshua was finding every hotspot Craig possessed. Though perhaps under Joshua's touch every part of Craig became a hotspot.

Perhaps Joshua was even going too slowly, a situation Craig hadn't realized could exist. With a man whose pride was to serve, perhaps Craig should have been a little more specific. Or, he could take the lead.

With a twist of his hips, Craig rolled Joshua to his back. Now was his time to torment, to nibble and to lick, to find places where Joshua could only squirm and enjoy. His ear made a wonderful playground, so did the edges of his lips. His neck, an even wider expense with that delicious strap muscle that he'd so delightfully tormented just a moment ago. Knowing what Joshua had done to him gave Craig a map of what to do in return.

Playing his lips over Joshua's stubbly cheek was a joy and a delight. The little rasping catches at his lips brought a puff of laughter from Craig's throat, a joy he didn't remember experiencing this decade. So long, so long, since the last time he'd found someone so wonderful that he had to peel their clothes off.

He could take his sweet time with cheek and ear, neck and collarbone, but perhaps that might be pushing Joshua's good nature to an extreme. He hadn't had the tantric experiences Craig had had, the ones he had taught himself so laboriously. Craig knew perfectly well how to extend his good time to absurd lengths, or perhaps to lengths that only Joshua would find absurd, but there was no need to test him.

Craig roamed lower, finding firm pecs topped with peaked nipples. Nipples that required teasing, tormenting, a lick and a suck. A lot of licks and sucks. Joshua's moans and small gasps every time Craig nibbled only spurred him to greater efforts. He might be here all day. Best way to spend the day, ever.

The light coating of hair on Joshua's chest needed a cheek rubbed against it. Or both cheeks. His lips, his nose. Joshua's chest needed to be experienced like a trampoline, or thousand-thread-count sheets, or the fur of a kitten, all wonder and joy.

"My turn." Joshua took command again, tipping Craig over to his back. Perhaps he could only use one hand to stroke lower, sweeping large expanses of Craig's body, but he made that one hand do double duty. Holding

Craig's ass, he gripped tightly just for a moment, upping the stakes. "Am I going too fast?"

"No, you're going just fast enough." Craig could draw this out all day, but touching Joshua at last made him want to rush. Craig never rushed.

Was it rushing if he wanted Joshua to take both of his buns in his hands and start prep for penetration? If Craig was okay with skipping intense investigations of abs and biceps, of the different scents at Joshua's neck, chest and groin, and skipping straight to the main event? If he was willing to give up three quarters of what he'd asked for and was getting, because the anticipation might kill him?

Joshua was making sure Craig would go with a smile on his face. For a guy who'd wanted to do some rushing himself, he was doing great with the slow. With dipping his tongue into the hollows at collarbone and neck. With scritching a light whisker tickle across the planes of Craig's chest. His stubble caught in Craig's chest hair, and the lightest of tugs made him shiver. So did the softness of lips on nipple, something Joshua approached with a wicked smile and tongue flickings.

The groan rumbled out of Craig from somewhere near his toes. Talk about worth the wait. Worth every second of finding out what kind of man Joshua was before their clothes came off. A thorough man, who took pride in what he did. Whatever he did. Who wanted to please and was fussy about whom he pleased.

He could please Craig all day long like this.

Although he'd probably change course if Craig begged.

Which was sounding like a really good idea. What with the casual brush of his arm over Craig's erection, pulsing with the beats of his heart and rising up to reach skin that probably wasn't meant to contact there and then. "Joshua, you could…," rumbled up through his throat unbidden.

"Yes, I could." The smartass with the magic tongue stopped long enough to talk. "I probably will, sooner or later." He laughed, deep and lascivious, sending a P-wave through Craig's lower body. "Right now I have things to lick. Let me know when I get to that spot where I could do the whatever."

Bastard went back to flicking the same nipple.

Had to be careful what he asked for, 'cause Joshua'd make sure he got it. Ohhhh…. Craig threaded his fingers through Joshua's thick hair. So tempting to tug his head down. A man could change his mind, right?

Not when Joshua's idea of what to do turned to a wet tracing of the ridges in Craig's abs. Closer, closer, yeah, getting closer. Maybe a little guidance….

Joshua skated his tongue right past the tip of Craig's cock, through the dip of muscle at his hip, and on to the ridge of bone. "Is this good?"

"Oh yeah." As if he couldn't tell, what with the soft whimpers Craig couldn't have stopped if he'd tried, and why would he? He lifted his hips, the better to fit flesh and mouth.

Might have been a mistake—Joshua grazed his teeth over the tender skin barely covering bone. "Oh, fuck."

"Not yet." Joshua laughed against skin. "Too intense?"

What would he do if Craig couldn't decide yes or no? Both words warred in his throat and came out as "Nggghngns."

That must be more no than yes—Joshua kept going. Craig could twist away. Or he could endure the nearly-too-much that somehow connected to every part of his body. Who'd think devotion to his hip—his fucking hip!— could bring him to the brink? Craig squirmed under Joshua's attentions, almost, not quite, bringing his cock to that busy, tormenting mouth.

"Nuh uh uh!" Joshua vaulted over Craig to capture his mouth, their hands entwined and pinioned over Craig's head. Instead of pressing body to body, Joshua hovered over Craig, only their cocks brushing lightly against each other. Swift touches as Joshua rocked over him, teasing him with the briefest of contact, lifting his ass to take that oh so desirable cock out of range when Craig thrust upward against him. Mouth to mouth was a sweet torment when cock to cock was only millimeters away. Craig thrust his tongue between Joshua's lips, wanting the fierce answer he could get only there.

What an answer it was. Joshua relented, dropping down to rest his weight against Craig. Chest to chest, belly to belly. Cock to cock.

At last. The full length of Joshua's body pressed against his. Everything he'd waited for, well, not everything, but closer than they managed to be yet.

Craig pulled his hands free, the better to wrap his arms across Joshua's back. To roam lower to find the delectable humps of his ass. Two marvelous mounds of muscle that flexed beneath his palms. His throbbing cock lay next to Joshua's stiff rod, trapped between their bellies. At last.

"We're going faster. Is this what you want?" Joshua asked.

"Yes. I want everything and I want it all at once." If Craig could have fifty hands, a dozen mouths and three cocks it would not be enough to be able to do all he wanted with Joshua.

"Let me think about how to give you everything and all at once." Joshua dove again to pull at Craig's earlobe with his lips. "I think we're doing pretty good so far though."

"Getting there," Craig gasped. "We might even get to the fucking part before sundown."

"That might be too fast," Joshua murmured. "You know I'm trying to give you exactly what you want."

Yes. Yes, he was. And doing a damn fine job of it.

A twist of the hips and Craig was on top. Joshua squeaked with surprise but rolled with him.

"So, you want to drive now?"

"Hell yes. My turn to make you crazy for a while." Craig could give as good as he got, and perhaps being active would make it easier to go as slow as he said he wanted. He could go faster slowly.

Craig's version of going slow involved licking a track down Joshua's chest. He flicked at both nipples, delighting in the pebbled texture under his tongue. Joshua's nipples must be as sensitive as his own—Joshua squirmed beneath Craig's tongue.

One good squirm deserved another. Craig had a hand as well and Joshua had another nipple. A little double trouble on his chest should keep them busy for a while, maintain the pace. The tender dark spot grew puffy, and Joshua found something to do with his own hands. Even if Craig was mostly out of range, Joshua still could caress head, shoulders, and hands. He stuck his finger into the circle of Craig's thumb and forefinger, a surprisingly erotic gesture. Pushing in and out, Joshua teased the webbing of Craig's hand, finding a stroke of fingertip to palm along the way.

"Did that just make you moan?"

"Uhhn." If Craig had ordered Joshua up from the concierge desk he couldn't have gotten a more perfect man. Not only did Joshua understand slow, but he was a man to laugh with in bed.

Craig spent as much time as Joshua had, perhaps even more, tracing his way down the beautiful ridges of abs and the dips of belly button and hip. If his own hip was nearly too sensitive to be teased, he'd find out the same for Joshua. Learning his new lover was a chorus of sighs and moans, of small gasps and grasps. Tightening his fingers in Craig's hair let him know every time he'd hit a tender spot. *All in good time* he told himself, but now was the time to find out what kind of commotion Joshua had been carrying around in his britches. The fat log that had showed through his suit trousers was naked and exposed now. Craig intended to make a very thorough exploration.

Starting with the delectable thin foreskin that covered the purplish glans. Craig sucked the skin into his mouth, tickling at every edge and surface with his tongue. Joshua cried out, tightening his hands in Craig's hair.

"Damn, that feels good," he gasped. "Keep doing that, I like it."

Craig would've responded, except that meant talking with his mouth full, and he wasn't about to let this wonderful erection go. Not when he could tease Joshua, not only by playing with the skin but by swiping his tongue around the head of the glans and probing the narrow slit that dripped bittersalt. Worth the wait, oh yes. Definitely worth the wait.

How long Joshua could tolerate this kind of play was an open question that Craig was desperate to answer, if only he could keep from plunging his mouth down on the firm shaft. Joshua's fine uncut cock throbbed between his lips. Enough for his mouth, enough for his hand, enough to play with for all time.

Spreading his legs, Joshua gave Craig access to everything he had. And Craig had another hand to cup Joshua's balls, to roll them gently inside the nubbly skin, covered with short clipped hair. Roaming further back, Craig trailed gentle fingertips across Joshua's taint, and who could say what was drawing the gasps and moans now? Perhaps he should try one thing at a time, but the glory of touching Joshua at last made him anxious. Anxious to try everything. All the things they talked about, that his new lover didn't really seem like he believed. Craig couldn't remember how much he told Joshua, aside from threatening to make him come half a dozen times before he blew his load.

Nobody ever believed it was possible the first time they tried it. Something from crazy videos and ancient texts, not something a real man could do. Craig had already done the impossible twice before breakfast. Joshua shouldn't doubt him on this. Maybe he should warn Joshua what he intended, or maybe just let nature take its course. Either way, they'd have fun.

The right course now was an enthusiastic blow job, something Craig enjoyed tremendously. He'd almost forgotten what it was like to be able to bring such exquisite pleasure to another man, let alone experiencing someone else's mouth. All the wonderful things that he could do for himself did not include "lips on own cock."

Note to self, Joshua loved getting blown. His cries and moans grew louder, and he slapped his hands to the mattress, where he gripped huge dents into the pillowtop. Was it a win if he could make Joshua put his fingers through the sheets?

"Craig, I'm gonna…"

Yes, he would, more than he could imagine. Craig dove down his shaft, hand at the base, fingertips at taint. If Joshua could….

"I'm really gonna…" was only encouragement to slide his tongue along the sensitive underside. "Craig!"

Craig shoved three fingertips against Joshua's taint, feeling the muscles there contract away from his prodding. With a tight grip at the base of Joshua's shaft, he rode out the shudders with his mouth sealed against Joshua's cock. Joshua tensed beneath his fingertips, and his entire body went rigid. He cried some wordless call of joy and did not fill Craig's mouth.

When Joshua relaxed and sank into the mattress, Craig dared release his grip.

"What the hell was that?" Joshua opened one eye.

To answer, Craig would have to let go. He lipped his way up, releasing his new lover's still-hard shaft to bounce against his firm belly. "Was it good?"

"Good doesn't begin to describe it." Joshua looked like he was made of jelly, all except the necessary. Craig grinned down at him.

"Tell me a little bit more about it." Had Joshua really accomplished what Craig thought he had?

"That was kind of weird actually. It felt so damn good, and then, well, it was different." Joshua panted a bit, reaching down to his balls. "It wasn't like any orgasm I'd had before. All inside. And I didn't shoot."

Sounded like Joshua was on the right track. "Would you like to have a lot of those?"

"I think I could get used to that." With his hands under Craig's armpits he brought him face-to-face and kissed him. "Do you want to explain?"

Not without kissing Joshua like he meant it. When he came up for air, he said, "That's what happens when you decouple your orgasm from your ejaculation. It's a tantric thing."

Joshua reached back down to his groin. "I thought that was a bunch of bullshit. And I'm still hard."

Everybody thought that at first, even Craig. "Both of those things can't be true at the same time, can they? I did say I wanted to make you come half a dozen times before you finally blew. Did you doubt I meant it?" Craig would help Joshua play with that firm column, but he didn't want to provide the overstimulation that would bring their play to a temporary halt.

"I should know not to doubt you. So far, you've done everything you said you'd do." With wrinkled brow, Joshua added, "I might have thought you were exaggerating about this, though."

"I don't exaggerate. I've been told 100 million times not to." Craig tried to swallow the snort that threatened to erupt while he waited for Joshua to pick up on the contradiction.

"Oh hell, I didn't think I was getting involved with a maker of bad jokes." His groan came from deep inside.

Craig laughed. "Too late now, you're stuck with me."

"Please don't tell me you leave the cap off the toothpaste, too." Joshua's hand continued its slow up-and-down journey. Didn't he believe he was still hard?

"We all have our little quirks. I bet you do something that'll drive me crazy too." Right now, Joshua's need to calm down and back a little farther from the brink was driving Craig mad. He wanted to rush, and even though the demand for going slow was his own, he was ready to throw it to the winds.

"I can't imagine what that would be. I'm the sweetest, most wonderful guy you'll ever meet." Joshua snickered.

He might even be right, even though he said it as a joke. Craig was willing to spend a lifetime finding out. They were doing good so far—what would Joshua do for turnabouts?

Chapter Nineteen

Mind completely blown.

Yes, Craig had promised multiple orgasms before a final climax, but Joshua had heard so much BS in his life, he'd only taken it for so much more bluster. A lot of guys talked a good game, with zilch to show for it. But what Craig had just helped him do was the real thing.

And here he was, feeling good and his dick not down, holding the most exquisite man. The man with the burgundy chocolate voice and the hands and mouth to match. The man who just brought Joshua to the heights and needed to get treated the same. Although he might've had some kind of climax during their play, and just hadn't said.

Didn't matter. Joshua had plans.

"Sooo, how are you doing on the slow thing?" Joshua pulled Craig closer. "Ready to speed things up just a little?"

"Maybe a little." Craig thrust his groin against Joshua's. Their hard cocks bumped, ridges catching each other. "But not too fast. What did you have in mind?"

"I think it's time for some lube." Getting to the lube required a long interval for more kissing and writhing. Oh, but this man felt good. With hugging and holding, and more nibbling on shoulders and neck. How had he managed to say no so often? And was he the stupidest man in the world for having said it at all? Or if there hadn't been so much no, would they have come to this new step in their lives? Because getting out of a bed that contained Craig was something Joshua only wanted to do once in a great while.

Eventually, Craig tore away long enough to reach to the bedside table and produce a bottle of lube and a condom. Which, what?

Hadn't Craig said it was years since…?

This didn't seem like the time to call bullshit, but apparently his face said more than his mouth did.

Craig noticed. "It keeps the toys clean."

Right. "Get comfy." Joshua drizzled his fingers. So Craig wanted to be on his belly, did he? With those luscious mounds of ass just begging to be nibbled, and his thighs spread. Damn, but he looked good, snuggled around the big down pillow and smiling so sexy over his shoulder.

The dark pucker between his cheeks twitched under Joshua's fingertips. "Um, slow is necessary here." Craig shut his eyes. "It's been… well, I go for toys with narrow necks."

"No problem." Kneeling between Craig's knees deserved to be savored. One finger, more lube. Push in, just a little farther. Craig was helping, that sped him up, but man, he was tight. But okay, because Joshua had a lot of fingers, a nearly full bottle, and all the time in the world. Time enough to go deeper, slip by slip, stroke by stroke. "Feeling good?"

"Yeah." Craig clenched on Joshua's finger. "Real good."

Oh, he was wet satin inside. Silky and full of nerve endings—Craig was starting to breathe harder. Good, good. Joshua slipped in and out at the rhythm of his own heart, in two, out two... The bedroom purr rumbling from Craig's throat needed to come up a notch—Joshua stroked the sweet spot on his way out.

Craig shivered and clenched again. "You... can do that all you like."

"Oh good. 'Cause I like, a lot." Oh man, did he. A handful of butt and a finger in weren't enough—Joshua stretched out over Craig, one leg thrown over Craig's, and never stopping his slow exploration. But he had to be close enough to kiss, even if Craig's face was pointed the other way.

He craned over his shoulder to reach, leaning into Joshua's chest. Their mouths didn't quite meet. Joshua rubbed his face against everything he could touch, and then slid down a little, the better to reach within and drop caresses at the Craig's nape. And talk.

"Toys with thin necks, hmm?" Joshua drew the tip of his tongue over the edge of Craig's ear. "Did you play with one of those toys while I was in the other bedroom?"

"Sure did." Reaching down, Craig found a handful of Joshua's thigh. "Every night you were there, and every night you weren't."

"Thinking about me?" A second finger would need more lube, and Craig hadn't said he was ready yet. Plus, Joshua would have to get up to grab the bottle, and he wasn't about to interrupt this tell-all session.

"You know it." Craig pushed back, brushing Joshua's cock with his butt. "Thought about you doing what you're doing now. Thought about your cock inside me, practically before we finished playing cards. Surprised me. A lot." Craig arched his back, drawing a deep suck of air through his nostrils. Sweet spot there, huh? When he relaxed enough to speak again— "Think I'm ready for another."

A second finger shouldn't come as a surprise. Joshua sat up to get the lube. Replenished, he handed the bottle to Craig. "We'll be needing that."

"Oh good." He lifted his butt to meet Joshua's hand.

Damn but this man looked fine, with his thighs parted to accept Joshua's fingers, his eyes closed in concentration. Joshua bent to drop kisses on the small of Craig's back, licking farther to crest on a muscular bun. He eased in and out of Craig's tight ring. "Tell me when you want another."

"Now would be good." Did that hiss mean "believe him" or "keep on with two"? Time to hedge bets—Joshua held out his other hand for Craig to squirt more lubricant, while keeping up his gentle but deep probing. Should he use both hands, or transfer the slick? Time spent pondering let him ease Craig's tightness that much more.

Two hands, how decadent. Joshua finally decided on adding his index finger while rubbing his thumb against Craig's taint. "You okay?" he asked when Craig quivered.

Took him a while to respond. "Oh yeah." Craig quivered again. "That's real good. And... I think... Come in. Please."

"Wait until you're asked" had become the asking. Joshua leaned down for a deep kiss that couldn't last forever—this time—he'd been asked to come in.

With his few ungreased fingers, he managed the condom and another generous splash of lube. And then—

He leaned down against Craig, hips fitting against ass, chest to back. Tip to hole. Nudging, pressing.

Craig groaned, "Yesssss...," and welcomed him in. "Josh, yeah, oh."

Yes. At last. In as deep as he could go. Into Craig, who wanted him there. And against all the odds, he was.

Joshua wrapped around Craig, twining their fingers together. Their mouths met kind of sideways, enough for kisses until they couldn't catch their breath. Whatever Craig was doing in there, it felt damned good, squeezing, and bringing full-body shakes. "Are you okay?"

The answer was a long time coming. "Wonderful." Craig twisted for another kiss. "Josh, just fuck me."

With an invitation like that...

Slow became fast, and slow again. Too wonderful to stop, too intense to continue. He pushed into this amazing man, every slap of their bodies a fresh wonder. When Craig shuddered, he stayed pressed in deep, letting him ride out the waves. Hope they felt as good from Craig's side as they did from his.

Even with best intentions, the sheer glory of what they did became too much—his balls drew up tight, and the gathering storm announced itself deep inside. "Craig, gonna..." mixed with "Yes, Josh!" and the world blew up.

They dozed in the slanting afternoon light, too spent to get up, unwilling to separate. When Craig rose on one elbow to gaze down on his new lover—his new lover! —all the wonders of the city outside paled in comparison to the man who shared his bed.

Joshua's eyes fluttered open. "Was that what you had in mind? I do strive to please."

Smartass. Craig rewarded the teasing with a kiss to the tip of Joshua's nose. "Better than I could have imagined."

That got a lifted brow. "Think what we could accomplish with some practice."

The thought toppled Craig to the pillow. "Um, yeah." He held Joshua tight, trying to imagine his life with lazy Saturday afternoons in bed together, or loving evenings after productive days, or even—a quickie before work? "Let's get right on that."

The chuckle rumbled up through Joshua's chest. "Gotta give me at least an hour to recover from what we just did."

"Me too," Craig admitted. "I think maybe even an hour and a half. That last one…"

"Last? Of how many?" That was some serious side-eye…

"Can't count that high. When you were in me, it all kind of ran together. I have serious spaghetti legs." A shower was out of the question for a while. The towel puppy had been unrolled for clean-up. Another way Joshua took care of their needs. Even if he didn't quite believe what Craig was telling him. That was okay. Once they had every night together….

"Speaking of practice." Joshua lifted his head to stare at his cock. "I thought with tantric stuff you lay there and brought yourself off with your mind. Like 3000-year-old new-age-y stuff."

"I suppose there has been a lot of nonsense grown up around it, but the practices do work if you take the time to learn them. It's just that immediate gratification is so much easier than discipline in the moment." Craig had spent a lot of whack-off sessions trying to force himself not to topple completely over the brink of orgasm. The learning curve had been a lot of fun.

"I guess you're onto something. What was that you did with your fingers on my taint?" Joshua turned them so that they lay side by side.

"I was trying to make you tense your PC muscles. Pubococcygeus—" He stumbled over the word. "—muscle. Guys have 'em too. That's where most of the control is." Craig kissed him. "The more you practice, the better you'll get at decoupling."

"I suppose I should expect something like that from an IT guy." Joshua kissed back and ran his hand down Craig's back to cup a buttock.

"Well, of course. That's what I do. Physiology is wetware, right? It's not prescientific mumbo-jumbo, it's neurons and impulses and muscular control. And the right kind of toys."

"Uh, just what kind of toys do you learn that on?" Okay, maybe Joshua believed a little.

"Aneros. They're designed to hit the prostate just so, with the narrow neck to more or less leave your hole out of it. And that handle… It gets your prostate from the taint side. I had to try several types, but the right shape and some practice works wonders." Good times. Joshua would enjoy finding out for himself. Craig would make sure of it.

"Huh. Never tried one of those. Wasn't sure which shape to get."

That was easy. "We'll get you an entire set and find out." Or maybe Craig could get over his weird territoriality about sharing his toys. Hadn't Joshua just put his dick in there? This being a couple thing might need some practice too.

"That's..." Huh, Joshua sputtered when he got flustered. Calling it cute out loud might not be wise, but it was cute. "Craig, that's too much."

"Really?" He leaned back up on one elbow to gaze into Joshua's face again. He drew lazy fingertips in swirls across Joshua's chest. "What's too much? Dropping a grand on sex toys? For you? Maybe buying you a private mountain before you marry me is too much, but mountains have to be carefully chosen. You can't store them in the bedside drawer."

"I don't have a bedroom drawer that big either," Joshua objected.

"Sure, you do. You just haven't seen it yet. It's in Colorado." Had Joshua forgotten where he was running to? "If you don't like my townhouse, we'll find a place you do like. Downtown maybe, so you feel at home? We have some buildings over thirty stories."

"Over thirty..." Joshua sounded faint. "Of course."

"You're still running toward me, right?" A cold shiver went through Craig's guts.

"Absolutely. Just—" Joshua pulled Craig down for a long kiss. "It'll take some mental adjustment to quit tripping over all the new. So, uh, what would you like to see today? We have about three hours before the Chinese restaurant opens."

That was really easy. "I have two choices, you pick from those." Yeah, their coming together had happened so fast, Joshua's head might be spinning as much as Craig's own. "I want to either see the finest packing store near your place or talk to that guy you know at Teterboro Airport. Because I'm buying either moving boxes or an airplane."

Craig forced himself to stillness while the gears in Joshua's head turned. He'd abide by whatever Joshua chose—his life had blown up, even if the pieces would fall into a pattern they both wanted.

The waiting was still hellish.

Finally, Joshua spoke. "I mostly have wardrobe to move. I think, maybe, five big boxes? And one for stuff. I'll leave the furniture with the sublet, I know someone trustworthy who wants to live in the neighborhood. I can be out of there…. Monday, even."

Craig bent to kiss his joy into Joshua's forehead. "That long? How about we go buy those boxes and I help you pack? Then you fly home with me tomorrow."

Joshua chuckled. "I'm good, but even I can't make a cargo company pick up on a Saturday night or Sunday morning."

Ah, logistical problems could be solved by waving money. Craig was all over that. "Sure you can. FedEx."

Sheer horror ran across his boyfriend's face. Craig could call him that now: they'd established the fact and were now settling details. However, save the endearment for when he wasn't staring bug-eyed.

"Craig! That's a thousand bucks a box!"

"So?" A rational objection if he was talking to anyone else, but something Craig had a lot of wasn't going to be a problem. It was just money, and money was a tool to get things done. Surely Joshua knew that, fulfilling whims for a living. Clearly he didn't see that Craig's resources covered him now.

Time to tell him again. "We can have it taken care of before we get to LaGuardia. We need to get you a ticket. I want to hold your hand all the way to Denver." Maybe he'd wear the Aneros for the flight. Between Joshua and the toy, it would be the best commercial flight ever.

Joshua still looked dubious. "I guess one of my room-mates could arrange for shipping, if it was all packed…."

Or not. Sounded like he wanted to see to his shipping himself, like he couldn't trust anyone else. So, okay.

"Nah. We'll take 'em to the airport with us. The airline flies great big planes with great big cargo holds. I'll buy the boxes their own damn tickets if I have to. Although they'll have to fly coach."

"Gotta draw the line somewhere," Joshua agreed faintly. "So, what do I put on my change of address form?"

Epilogue

Joshua pulled up in the parking lot of the Darya Cafe, willing his hands to unclench from the steering wheel. Driving was still such a new skill. Denver might have the occasional traffic jam, which he preferred to endure from the back of a car someone else drove, or the passenger seat of Craig's new 7-series BMW. He'd grown up depending on public transportation, of which Denver had a quarter of what he was used to, or walking, which seemed to take everyone in Colorado by surprise.

He learned to drive, as much as it scared him, mostly to please his lover. Craig wanted to put him in wheels, but the Mercedes GLA 250 would have tied Joshua in anxious knots. He'd insisted on nothing fancier than a three-year-old Ford Escape with disposable bodywork for his first-ever vehicle, and agreed to the leather upholstery only because it came with the fenders.

Learning to drive under Craig's tutelage was just one challenge they faced in the last nine months. Craig had never expected to teach anyone, and learning to teach had been his challenge. They gotten past the shouty "No! Stop!" stage fairly fast, but the experience had shaken them both.

Faced with more free time than he'd ever imagined, Joshua had put the hours to good use. As "concierge for two" he'd learned the ins and outs of this new city, making friends, influencing people, and finding all the interesting nooks and crannies.

Like this restaurant. The place had been not five miles distant from Craig's business for the last… Oh… As long as the business had existed. Nor had Craig realized that halal restaurants would cater to his dietary needs as well as the kosher establishments did. There would be *baba ghanoush* and *ghormeh sabzi* tonight, foods that Craig had never tasted and Joshua missed.

His lover reached across from the passenger seat to cup his hand around Joshua's. "You did great. Was it really that bad?"

Craig had no idea. Maybe he was comfortable with the idea of propelling a 3000-pound weapon through the hurtling masses of other multi-thousand-pound weapons, but Joshua was only too conscious of holding his life and Craig's in the palms of his hands. "I'm glad we waited until after 7 o'clock. I'd rather miss the traffic."

"But you drove like a champ." Craig left off the patting to cup his hand around Joshua's neck and pull him sideways across the console for a kiss. "I knew you could do it."

Doing it and enjoying it were two different things. "It'll be easier going home, or… Maybe not. I still don't like driving in the dark." Everything looked different in the dark.

Except Craig. Craig looked fine: day, night, clothed, unclothed, behind his desk, in the gym, the kitchen, or the bedroom. Joshua didn't think he'd ever get tired of looking.

Which didn't solve the problem of driving home. He'd have to see how his courage held up.

"We should probably decide now, so we know which one of us is going to have a drink with dinner."

"Neither one of us is going to have a drink with dinner, because this restaurant doesn't have a liquor license. It goes with the halal food." If Joshua drove home tonight, he'd need a stiff one once they got home.

He'd want a stiff one anyway, but not in a glass. He'd be going home with Craig. To the enormous townhouse in the southern end of the city where Craig lived before Joshua made the trek west.

Joshua still wasn't convinced they needed a living room the size of the Vivaldi's lobby, but hey, they had that kind of space, and he'd had almost gotten used to it. He'd also gotten used to a bedroom twice the size of his entire apartment in Manhattan. His clothes closet was larger than his share of the space in his old apartment. He really didn't miss a bathroom whose walls he could touch by just by extending both arms.

On the other hand, sharing a postage stamp of a home with Craig would be just fine too, which was about as much of the house as was habitable when he moved in. Whatever vision of his future inspired Craig to buy a four thousand square foot home with four bedrooms hadn't inspired him to decorate, or buy much furniture beyond a bedroom suite and a couple of pieces of art. The kitchen table was Ikea's finest, and it did keep the plates off the floor. Joshua had tried howling in the near-empty living room to see if it echoed. It did.

Craig had caught him testing the acoustics. "Find us

a decorator," he said, and dropped a quarter of a million bucks into the household account. Joshua was still spending the money, but they had couches and rugs and a solid maple table now.

"You're sure this place is okay?" Craig's other hand went to his inner jacket pocket, where the yellow lifesaver of epinephrine rode every day. Joshua had one in his pocket too. They hadn't needed to jab Craig since the fateful party, but still, constant vigilance.

"I checked the menu, I checked the dietary rules, and you should be just as safe here as you would in your own kitchen. Not a shrimp to be found." Joshua turned to find Craig's lips. "I wouldn't risk you. I kinda love you."

"It's *our* kitchen. And I kinda love you too."

Maybe a smoochfest in the parking lot of the Middle Eastern restaurant wasn't the best idea they'd ever had, or maybe it was. The deep tinted windows on the Escape provided enough privacy.

Joshua evaded the twenty-seventh kiss to say, "I hope you're hungry."

"I'm always hungry for you. Yeah, I know, that's the corniest thing to come out of my mouth all day." Craig laughed.

Joshua had to agree, but it was still nice to be wanted. Best of all, Craig seemed to want him even more than he had at the beginning. "How about we go inside and put something into your mouth?"

"Sounds good to me." Craig met him in front of the SUV. "You could have driven the BMW."

No way. "Maybe next year. If I'm going to destroy any fenders, it shouldn't be on your pretty sedan." Two long scratches along the Escape's rear quarter panel attested to Joshua's inexperience.

Why did Craig perk up so much at the promise of destruction?

Fabulous smells making delicious promises greeted them at the door of the restaurant. Joshua inhaled by the mouthful. His recent adventures in the kitchen hadn't included anything of this cuisine, but he could get another cookbook and begin his experiments. The Viking range at home had seen a lot more action since Joshua moved to town. Craig whipped up their Sunday morning omelets and toasted the late-night grilled cheese sandwiches, but Joshua had taken to a kitchen where he didn't have to dodge three other people and fight for refrigerator space.

Craig had eaten all of his experiments, the raw and the burnt, the successful and the flop, with thanks to the chef. Even though the chef had started cooking as a way to fill his suddenly unscheduled days, being able to feed Craig with his own hands and efforts was weirdly satisfying.

Tonight Joshua wanted to put the fate of their dinner into the hands of pros, because he had something he wanted to tell Craig. Not a time to trust himself with a knife.

Craig glanced up from behind his menu. "I don't even know where to start."

"Do you want me to choose?" Echoes of dinner at Shoshana's teased at his tongue.

"Yes. Please do." Craig scanned the descriptions anxiously as Joshua made suggestions.

Perhaps Craig would feel less adversarial toward his food once he was sure it wouldn't try to kill him. Poor guy, dinner at a new restaurant was the kind of adventure where he wasn't sure that everyone would come home alive. They'd never gotten a valid explanation for the lobster vol a vents at the IPO party.

Over pita chips and eggplant dip, Craig gradually relaxed, enough to start talking about his day. Joshua had only the vaguest of understanding of the threats to cybersecurity that Craig planned to fight with his new release, but understood "major new client" quite well. "You plan to launch this by the end of the year?"

Craig nodded. "The client's been hacked twice with their current set up, so the sooner the better. For them and for us."

"Sounds like that's going to keep you very busy for quite some time." He had to get a feel for this, because he wouldn't risk disrupting Craig's project by scheduling personal events during a particularly hectic period.

"I'm always busy. But I hire engineers and code jockeys to do the actual work." He ate another dollop of baba ghanoush. "Although I do have another project roughed out, which might eat up the spare hour here and there."

"Oh really?" What else would Joshua have to dodge?

"There's no real timeline on this project. It's more of a labor of love. On steroids, because it's mixed with a labor of hate." Good thing that evil chuckle wasn't directed at Joshua.

"Oh really?" What else could he possibly say to that?

The waiter came by to deposit fragrant plates of spicy braised beef, roasted lamb, grilled vegetables, and rice. Craig took an appreciative sniff. "This is going to be good." He glanced up at Joshua. "My noncompete agreement is about to expire. Nothing like a grudge, knowledge, and good capitalization to kickstart a new venture. A new/old venture, you might say."

"Students everywhere, rejoice?" Joshua hadn't forgotten Craig's textbook project.

"Possibly professors everywhere rejoice, too." Craig lost the plot with his first forkful of the *ghormeh sabzi*. He closed his eyes and savored the second bite of beef, swallowing reverently. When he came to himself, three mouthfuls later, he stopped to admire the saffron rice. "Oh, this is wonderful. We're going to have to come back and eat our way down the menu."

"Works for me." Dare he risk distracting Craig with a taste of his lamb? Could he duplicate this at home? Lemon, mint... "Back to the professors. Why are they rejoicing?"

"Publish or perish hasn't gone away." Craig glanced up from his plate. "Back during my first incarnation of hawking textbooks, I relied a great deal on public domain work. Now I'm thinking custom textbooks. Official publications, in their field of interest, perfect for using in their classes. Offered on a rental basis to endlessly refreshed supplies of students. At a much higher pay scale than academics are used to seeing for their publications. Since I think some of them are fortunate to see twelve cents per copy the traditional way. Think we could get any of them interested?"

"I think you could get quite a lot of them on board with that." Joshua chuckled around a mouthful of figs and couscous. "Convincing professors to contribute a chapter or two should be much simpler than coaxing a maître d' into giving my clients a table when the restaurant was full."

"Perhaps I should put you in charge?" Craig's eyebrows went up.

Oh, no. "I don't know a thing about the textbook field, or tech, or cyber-commerce. Putting me in charge would be a recipe for disaster." A man had to know his own limits.

"Of author contacts." Craig amended his scope. "You know more than anyone about finding the right people for a job and then getting them to do it. If it's experts on art history instead of dry cleaning or dog dyeing, is that so different?"

"Not really," Joshua admitted slowly. If he asked a local expert in a field who they thought the five next best experts were, and then asked those five for their opinions, he could have a good pool of candidates, and some of them were bound to be interested...

Had he just agreed to do this, even in his head? He could schmooze with the best of them, and nine months of self-defined goals had him starting to invent projects. "When does the noncompete expire?"

"About three months from now." Craig's evil grin went hesitant. "A lot of noncompetes expire around then."

Part of Joshua's year's leave of absence had involved promising not to work for any other New York hotel. It had been the price for all the other concessions Grant Wetzel made, and since Joshua was headed to Denver, conceding that point was nothing at all. "I know. I've been meaning to talk to you about that."

Joshua hadn't threatened their new kitten — why did Craig look like Joshua had waved a knife at Muffin?

"It's nothing bad, really, Craig. It's just, I was looking

at the terms of my noncompete and need to know if I can do certain things here in Denver without violating it." Hadn't Craig figured out that Joshua was in this for the long haul? He wouldn't get a kitten with just anyone.

The tension went out of Craig's shoulders. "What is it that you want to do? Has one of the local hotels made you an offer?"

He had talked to the concierges at the local four and five-star hotels, but mostly for information gathering. If you already knew who knew the best of the best to be had in the area, why not pick their brains? Joshua was done with his time in hotel lobbies except as a guest. Unless... "Did you want me to apply?"

"You're so busy now, I don't know how you ever had time to hold a job." Craig paused with a forkful of meat halfway to his mouth. "I suggested being part of the textbook project because asking a busy man to do something means it gets done. But that's up to you. I settled a chunk of SecurNow stock on you so you'd never *have* to apply anywhere."

Craig had taken him to the lawyer's office the same morning the lock-out period expired, and informed him nothing actually needed his signature, so shut up and accept it. A week wasn't long enough to get used to the idea.

"I am always busy, but so far it's been learning the new turf. And... I may have made a commitment or two about helping." Joshua took a deep breath, because there wouldn't be a better time than now to bring this up to Craig. "There's a small foundation which is doing some really good work with the local LGBT kids, and they've run into fiscal problems."

"Should I write them a check?"

"That part's up to you." Craig could probably solve all their problems with three lines of chicken scratch, but that wasn't what Joshua had in mind. "What I'm actually thinking is to host a fundraiser on their behalf. I'm talking a very small foundation, with a reach that isn't likely to put this into the debutantes' ball category for size. I could probably find a restaurant or hotel venue, but that would put such a dent into the profits that it wouldn't do the foundation enough good. Not enough to keep their day shelter open." Joshua took a deep breath, knowing that Craig had to sign off on this. "What I'd really like to do is to keep the expenses down by hosting it. At our place."

That got Craig's gears turning. "Is our place ready to host?"

"Pretty nearly. We can rent quite a lot of what we need for the actual event. The caterers can use the kitchen as it is, and all seafood stays far, far away. In fact, I could arrange all the purchases through known safe outlets." Joshua had put quite a lot of thought into this, because helping others could absolutely not risk Craig. The misadventure at the Morgenthau Pierce affair would not be permitted to repeat in their own home.

"It's your home too, Joshua. If you want to do this, do it. Tell me where to be when, and what to wear, and I'll be there." Craig dropped his fork onto his empty plate. "Not sure why you were so hesitant to tell me."

"I—" There hadn't been a lump in Joshua's throat a moment ago. "It… just seems like something Felicity might have come up with. And I know how you felt about that."

Craig snorted hard enough to puff a grain of rice off his plate and into his lap. "That's nothing at all like what Felicity had in mind. There's a big difference between being on the board of directors of the 'right' charities for the seen and be seen factor, compared to doing something good in the world because it needs doing." The handwritten tab's edge moistened in the condensation from his tea glass. Craig dropped his credit card over the inked numbers. A waiting server scooped it up and bustled away. "I won't even suggest you ask her for advice."

"I don't care to be incinerated with a glance, so no." Felicity got along with Joshua best by not being in the same place at the same time, and Craig didn't ask it of them often enough to strain the professional composure Joshua could maintain in the face of three Felicities and two ringing telephones. "The foundation people do seem to know what they're doing. They just lost a couple of major benefactors though."

"That ought to be fixable now that Hannes and Ridley have taken an interest." Craig scribbled on the credit card tab, his pen dipping into the deep scratch in the wooden table. "When did you think to throw this shindig?"

"Given the lag time on good furniture, plus getting things organized and invitations out, maybe four months from now. Not sooner." Joshua mentally added "postage" to his to-do list and tucked his chair under the table.

"Let's do it." Snagging the mints the waiter had left on the table with the tab, Craig traded Joshua a candy for car keys. "Four months is after the end of your leave of absence. Is that going to create a problem?"

"Only if planning steps on my noncompete. Or if the Vivaldi thinks I'm really coming back." Oh! Was that what Craig had been so jumpy about? If his sweetie was feeling insecure, time to take him home fast, and then take him extra slow in bed. And turn the tables. "You do plan to keep me?"

"Forever and a day, fella. Wouldn't have put you on the credit card if I hadn't." Craig turned on the engine, but let his hand drop away from the gearshift without putting the SUV into reverse. "Um, you're supposed to use it now and again for more than just groceries, you know?"

Maybe it was misplaced pride that he hadn't. "I know, but my needs are simple and my wants are few." He covered Craig's hand with his own, a small touch in the near dark of the parking lot. "And you already take care of most of them."

Spreading his fingers to catch Joshua's in a grip reminiscent of their favorite sex position, Craig murmured, "I try. You take care of mine."

"I try." A shudder ran through Joshua—if he clenched just so, the way Craig taught him, he could... Well, he wanted to save the best for home with his lover. "So, do you think before we ramp up full scale on the new projects, we could take a week off for a trip?"

"Sure. What do you have in mind?"

"New York. I'm going to stretch the leave of absence to the last possible degree, but I really should turn up to sign my exit papers in person." How else would Joshua see the look on Grant Wetzel's face? He'd barely survived the assorted purges Angry Stockholder had instigated. Just seeing Joshua ought to turn Grant's face an interesting shade of puce, particularly if he was allowed to think, just for a moment, that Joshua was coming back. "And I'd like to show you around the city."

Craig gripped Joshua's fingers more tightly and held the squeeze. "I'd love for you to show me the city."

Joshua had a long list of places to take his lover. "It would make up for showing you nothing but a packaging store last time."

"That was exactly the scenery I wanted then." Craig leaned over the console in a whiff of leather and stole a kiss. "But for an anniversary trip, yeah, we could take a non-emergency helicopter ride around the Statue of Liberty."

Not precisely what Joshua had in mind, but he'd add that to the itinerary, since Craig suggested it.

"Do you want to stay at the Vivaldi?" Craig asked. "Making faces at the bellmen is optional."

"Making faces wouldn't be any fun if it wasn't Henry," Joshua pointed out. "And he got canned."

"Good riddance!" So Craig wasn't entirely over his anger at Henry—his fist had tightened enough to squish Joshua's fingers. "But let's stay in the Central Park Suite and walk through the lobby holding hands. The way it ought to be."

"I'll hold your hand any time, but... One of the one-bedroom suites would be fine. Or a regular room." Joshua would absolutely not sleep in the second bedroom this time around, so why even rent it?

"Maybe I want to hear you play the piano. Come on, Joshua, I want us to have a redo on staying there together, no sneaking around like we're doing something wrong." The plea in Craig's deep, smooth voice sent shudders through Joshua. "We weren't then, and we sure as hell aren't now. I want them to acknowledge you as a guest."

"If that's what you want, that's what we'll do." Wouldn't take more than a couple calls to find out who was on the front desk when…

Craig jerked Joshua out of his calculations by taking his hands back. He started the engine, chuckling. "And don't worry about scoring a sweetheart deal like last time. I want us in that suite. You need to remember you have a wealthy husband."

That joke again.

No, what he had was a wonderful man who used money as a tool. Who loved him. And who Joshua loved back. Maybe, down the road, their soon to be party-worthy living room would be a good place to invite friends and make some promises.

"Yeah." Joshua wouldn't spoil his lover's jest by arguing about which part mattered—Craig already knew. He draped his arm over the seat back so he could play with a lock of Craig's hair. Craig leaned into his hand, pointing the little vehicle toward home. Their home. "Yeah, I do."

About the Author

P.D. Singer lives in Colorado with her slightly bemused husband, one young adult, and thirteen pounds of cats. She's a big believer in research, first-hand if possible, so the reader can be quite certain Pam has skied down a mountain face-first, been stepped on by rodeo horses, acquired a potato burn or two, and will never, ever write a novel that includes sky-diving.

When not writing, playing her fiddle, or skiing, she can be found with a book in hand.

Follow the adventures at Pam's website (http://pdsinger.com).

Sign up for the Rocky Ridge Books mailing list for new releases, news, and tidbits from P.D. Singer, Eden Winters, Z. Allora, DH Starr, and Cari Z.

Also by P.D. Singer

Spokes

Pro cyclist Luca Biondi lives for the race. For the star of Team Antano-Clark, victory lies within his grasp—if he can outdistance 200 other hopefuls, avoid suspicion from race officials, and keep his lieutenant more friend than foe. Luca also has secrets, and eyes for amateur cyclist and journalist Christopher Nye.

Christopher understands Luca's need to keep their relationship under wraps, but chafes at hiding in the shadows of his lover's career. He's ready to cheer Luca's victories, but he knows too well how triumph can turn to tears. While Christopher's heart sees Luca the man, his inner journalist—and his editor—sees the cycling world's biggest scoop.

From the jagged curves of the Colorado Rockies to the viciously steep Belgian hills, Luca can ride out any bumps—except rumors.

A few words in the wrong ear could crash everything. With miles between them, hints of scandal, and Luca's fierce need to guard his reputation, a journalist might have to let go of the biggest story of his career or risk forcing his lover to abandon the race. Christopher and Luca face a path more treacherous than any road to the summit in the Italian Alps.

A New Man

Senior year of college is for studying, partying, and having fun before getting serious about life. Instead, Chad's days are filled with headaches and exhaustion, and his fencing skills are getting worse with practice, not better. Then there's his nonexistent love life, full of girls he's shunted to the friend zone. Is he asexual? Gay?

Grad student Warren Douglas could be out clubbing, but his roommate is better company, even without kisses. He's torn up watching Chad suffer, gobbling ibuprofen and coming home early on Friday nights. If Chad weren't straight, Warren would keep him up past midnight. They're great as friends. Benefits might answer Chad's questions.

A brief encounter with lab rats reveals Chad's illness—he needs surgery, STAT, and can't rely on his dysfunctional parents for medical decisions. Warren's both trustworthy and likely to get overruled—unless they're married. "You can throw me back later," Warren says, and he may throw himself back after his husband turns out moody and hard to get along with, no matter how much fun his new sex drive is. Chad's a new man, all right…

…but Warren fell in love with the old one.

And more...

Novels
    The Rare Event
    A New Man
    Diving Deep
    Fire on the Mountain
    Snow on the Mountain
    Fall Down the Mountain
    Blood on the Mountain
    Return to the Mountain
    Spokes
    Otter Chaos
    Two Bears and a Baby

Novellas
    Donal _agus_ Jimmy
    Prep Work
    Tail Slide

Selected Shorts
    Cross the Mountain
    O'Carolan's Seduction
    Training Cats
    On Call: The Collection
    Set Up

www.ingramcontent.com/pod-product-compliance
Lightning Source LLC
Chambersburg PA
CBHW020407210626
46816CB00006BB/2158